COMING ATTRACTIONS

Stories by Sharon Butala, Bonnie Burnard & Sharon Sparling

Acknowledgements: "The Chinese Coat" by Sharon Sparling originally appeared in *Saturday Night*.

ISBN 0 88750 496 5 (hardcover)
ISBN 0 88750 497 3 (softcover)

Cover art by Maxwell Bates courtesy Canada Council Art Bank. Book design by Michael Macklem.

Printed in Canada

PUBLISHED IN CANADA BY OBERON PRESS

It has now been four years since Oberon began publishing a companion volume to *Best Canadian Stories*. The idea behind the series has been to introduce talented and committed new writers—who may have previously been published only in small or regional literary magazines—to a wider audience while offering them a more complete exposure than the alternative of a one-story appearance in *Best Canadian Stories*. The first collection was called *First Impressions* and was followed in successive years by *Second* and *Third Impressions*. This fourth edition of the anthology is marked by a change in editors and a change of title: from now on the series will be known as *Coming Attractions*.

This year the stories are by Sharon Butala, Bonnie Burnard and Sharon Sparling. It is not significant that they are all women or that two of them come from Saskatchewan. What is important is that each of them is a thoughtful, imaginative writer able to transcend real or imagined experiences and translate them into fiction of the first rank.

Sharon Butala was born in Saskatchewan and wrote her first novel when she was nine, followed by a play a year later. She wrote nothing more for the next 25 years until after her second marriage in 1976 when she finally had "the freedom and the opportunity" to write. Two years later Butala sent her first story to *Western People,* a supplement of the mass-circulation newspaper *The Western Producer,* and it was published. "Everybody reads the *Producer* around here," says Butala.

She divides her time between a ranch in the extreme southwest corner of the province and a hay farm "just outside Eastend and 30 miles closer to civilization." As any reader of "The Mission" and "Breaking Horses" will know, she is thoroughly familiar with farm life. "I *love* living in the country—in this country anyway," she says.

Butala considers writing short stories a training ground for novels. She has completed a full-length manuscript that will be published by Fifth House of Saskatoon in early 1984 and is at work on the first draft of a second novel. She was one of three winners in the Saskatchewan Writers' Guild Long Fiction competition in 1982 and she has been published in *Saskatchewan Gold,* an anthology of stories written by local writers. Not a bad list of credentials in a seven-year writing career from a person who believed that "the arts belonged to the upper classes."

Bonnie Burnard was born and raised in southwestern Ontario and has lived in Saskatchewan for the last nine years. She began writing nearly four years ago after her last child was born. "Saskatchewan," says Burnard, who also has a story in *Saskatchewan Gold,* "must be the easiest place in the world for a new writer to begin. The Saskatchewan Writers' Guild and the Summer School of the Arts at Fort San (funded by the Saskatchewan Arts Board) provide a very solid structure."

About her work Burnard says: "I write because I have been, for as long as I can remember, surprised, appalled, moved, disgusted and impressed with what people, myself included, will do. Even those who think they have a firm grip on some humane pattern of behaviour cannot always isolate themselves from those who do not, or from circumstances that usurp their control. This is not news, of course, but it is, I think, my motivation. A good short story traps human behaviour as a picture can.

"I had some notion of what I wanted to address with each of these stories, but the themes changed as I was writing them. In "Grizzly Mountain" the story of a boy thrown off as relationships dissolved became, I think, a story about people connecting in an indirect, unintentional way. The force of emerging sexuality in "Crush" changed into something about the lack of connection, about the way people live their own stories and use each other as characters. Opposed personalities in a marriage in "Reflections" became some kind of examination of love and how it comes in bits and pieces rather than as a state or condition and how it often fails as a protection."

Anybody reading Sharon Sparling's "The Chinese Coat" and "A Hinge of Possibilities", would suppose that she was, at the very least, an accomplished amateur pianist. Not so. "I regret to tell you," she says, "that my musical experience consists of singing in the bath. I have a rich fantasy life," she adds.

Sparling is the youngest of the three writers published here and a native of Montreal. She has a degree from McGill in Theatre Arts and is currently working on a

Masters in English at Concordia. As part of her program she is taking a creative writing course from the novelist and short-story writer Elizabeth Spencer. It was Spencer who encouraged her to send us "The Chinese Coat", which had previously been published in *Saturday Night*.

Sparling has been writing seriously for only two years. To date she has written short stories exclusively, but she's planning a novel.

Here then are stories from three talented and exciting writers, a promise of more, much more, to come.

SANDRA MARTIN

SHARON BUTALA

BREAKING HORSES

Edna watches the horsebreaker cross the yard with her husband. Stan is tall and lean, almost thin, and he walks as if he thinks the barn may possibly be on fire, but is too polite to run. The horsebreaker, Chuck, is average height, but stockier, in no hurry. They are both wearing chaps and spurs and heavy parkas. The wind is up. A November blizzard is blowing in from the west, but already Edna can see that it will be a dry blizzard blowing more dirt than snow. Anyway, she knows, it won't stop anything; not the calf-weaning, not the horsebreaking, not the eternal slope of the hills to the west that block her view of nothing, not the watchful tension of Stan's face.

I am 40 this year, Edna reminds herself as she watches the horsebreaker and her husband cross the corral.

All day the horsebreaker has crossed and recrossed in front of the kitchen window, his big back moving up and down in a cautious rhythm. His face is shadowed by the fur of the parka's hood. His hands are hidden in leather mitts; chaps hide his legs. She has seen him pass in front of her view six, ten, a million times, and now evening has crept up on them again.

After the dishes are done she sits down in the living-room in front of the TV. Stan is asleep in his chair. The horsebreaker is lying on his back on the floor. He begins to do situps. Between situps he talks to her.

"She left me," he says as he rises, "for an Indian." He drops back down again quickly. The muscles of abdomen unfold. "An Indian!" He rises half-way, grimacing, and holds for a second. "Took the kids," grunting as if he wanted to say more. Edna pulls her legs into the chair. Her hands grip its arms. The horsebreaker speeds up. He is like a clock, up and down, up and down, a crazed clock with unnatural speed: tickety-tock, tickety-tock. "Fifty," he says, and stops. He swivels on his bottom to look at her. "I was in Calgary," he says. "Drunk. I didn't care. I was driving downtown and I couldn't decide where to go, see? Made a U-turn doing 50 right on the main street. I just didn't care." He stands up and begins to do knee bends balancing on one foot. After a while he does them balancing on the other foot. Edna watches him. She thinks how perfect his body is. His shirt is open and she can see the curly black hair that grows on his chest. It is wet with sweat. It crosses her mind that her kids are grown up and gone, that nobody can take them away.

"I didn't make enough money to suit her," he says, panting as he bobs up and down. Stan has wakened.

"She was no good, a bitch," he says. "You're better off without her."

"But my kids," the horsebreaker gasps.

"You're just rid of grief ten years sooner," her husband says. This makes Edna angry, but she doesn't say anything. The small room has begun to take on a dampness, a faint, salty odour from Chuck's exertions. She would like to see his rage played out. She would like to see him smile. She would like the horsebreaker to look at her with his bright blue eyes. She rubs her moist palms carefully on her thighs. She can feel the heat in her cheeks and hopes she isn't blushing. No, she thinks, she would never do that.

Chuck finishes his exercises, goes outside to the toilet. When he comes in a moment later, he says, "Well, time for bed," although it is only nine o'clock. He goes and washes and soon the house smells of liniment. All night Edna smells it as she weaves in and out of dreams.

Edna puts on her ragged yellow jacket that she wears to do barn chores or to ride with Stan. She ties a blue scarf under her chin and goes outside. She crosses the yard and goes to sit on the corral. Inside the corral Stan and the horsebreaker are just about to untie the gelding that lies on his side on the frozen ground, all four feet trussed. They put a halter on him and loop a rope around his neck. They put a rope through the halter and then the horsebreaker goes in and carefully unties the ropes around his feet, leaping back out of the horse's way. For a long moment, the horse doesn't move. It is as if he doesn't realize that he has been untied. Then he rocks to his feet, whinnies and tries to run. Stan and the horsebreaker both hold onto the rope that ends around his neck. They dig their heels into the ground and lean back. The gelding drags them slowly. When he stops to rear they quickly loop the rope around the snubbing-post several times and the horsebreaker runs and jumps onto his saddle horse, which has been standing quietly by the barn. The gelding pulls on the rope and when he can't free himself this way, rears, twisting his neck. Edna can see the whites of his eyes as they roll back in fear. He rears again and again until finally, he falls. The horsebreaker takes the rope from Stan, who has unwound it from the snubbing-post, and wraps it around his saddle horn. The horse is still lying on its side, its four legs stretched straight out, its ribs heaving up and down. Stan goes over to it and hits it on the flank with his rope. The horse rolls to its knees and thrusts itself upright with its powerful back legs. It tries to run, and is brought up short by the rope. Chuck's horse digs in, then backs up slowly, trying to keep the rope taut, jerking the gelding into a turn. Stan, keeping a careful eye on the two horses, walks over to where Edna sits on the coral, and says, "He'll be on him by tomorrow."

The gelding is black with one white spot on his face and a flick of white on one pastern. His mane and tail are black too. His coat is beginning to lengthen and he has a shaggy look about him. Edna remembers when he was slicked off for summer and shone like coal. He is following behind Chuck's horse now, only balking now and then, or twisting his neck. Stan walks behind with his rope ready to hit him on the rump if the horse balks or rears.

Edna shivers. She climbs down off the corral and goes back to the kitchen.

There is a letter from Merrilee, their oldest daughter, in the mail. Billy, their oldest son, works on the oil rigs in Alberta; Larry rides on a government lease south of them; Lucy, married at sixteen, lives in a town a hundred miles away with her mechanic husband and their three children. Only Merrilee writes. Merrilee is a model in Calgary.

Stan holds his face expressionless while he reads the

letter. Then he tosses it onto the table and makes a sound, perhaps a grunt, or maybe a snort. He goes outside. Edna picks up the letter and reads it.

"Dear Mom and Dad," Merrilee writes. "I am thinking of moving to Vancouver. There are more opportunities for models there, and I am getting tired of Calgary. I managed to lose another two pounds last week, Mom. I have stopped going out with Hans. Last night I went to a really fancy new restaurant. The waiters and waitresses were all dressed in togas. You would have loved it, Mom. I think I'll leave for Vancouver at the end of the month. I'll try to get home before I go, but don't expect me. Love, Merrilee."

After Edna has read it, she puts the letter down and walks to the sink where she begins to wash the dishes. She is crying. While she waits for the tears to stop, she continues to wash the dishes. The horsebreaker, who has been with them a week now, comes in for a drink of water and sees that she is crying. He hesitates in mid-step, then looking at her as if he is seeing her for the first time, asks, "Is something the matter?"

"No," Edna says, and then laughs at the silliness of this. He looks puzzled for a moment, but then he grins back at her as if her behaviour is not unexpected. He pats her back awkwardly as he goes by to the door. When his hand is on the doorknob, he looks at her again. She notices how perfect his jawline is, a clean masculine line, but with a delicate quality. After a long moment, he opens the door and goes outside.

"She should be married," Stan says to her in a low voice. "You keep encouraging her."

"I wanted something better for her. That's all," Edna answers. She turns away, but he pulls her back toward him, one hand on her bare shoulder where the strap of her nightgown has slipped down. They stare at one another.

"I'm afraid of what she does," he says, letting his hand drop to his side.

"She's a model," Edna insists. "Models get paid well. They go out with lots of men. Merrilee is beautiful," she adds. Stan lies down on their bed and stares at the ceiling.

"Maybe," he says. Edna lies down on her side of the bed.

"Look at Lucy," Edna says after a while. They lie side by side not speaking. Edna says to the ceiling, "I meant for Merrilee to get an education. You know that."

"Two months in nursing and she quits to go to modelling school. I blame you," he says to Edna. "You filled her with ideas how nothing around here was good enough for her." Then he turns over so that his back is to her. She wants to say, "But what's wrong with modelling? What's wrong with it? At least she isn't stuck on some god-forsaken ranch somewhere. At least she doesn't have three kids at nineteen, like Lucy, like me." But instead, she turns her back on Stan and tries to sleep.

Edna sees that it is past ten and nobody has come for morning coffee. She takes it off the stove and fills the thermos. Through the window she can see the horsebreaker riding at a lope in big figure eights. She watches for a moment, and then impulsively she jerks her jacket off the hook, puts it on, and takes the thermos outside. She stands just to one side of the invisible figure eight he is making. He glances away from the horse long enough to take in the thermos.

"I'll ride him to the corral," he calls to her. She follows them over to the corral where the horsebreaker hobbles the gelding. As he comes toward her, she sees the sweat trickling down beside his ears from his hair. He takes the filled thermos cap from her. He is panting slightly, and takes a deep breath before he sips the hot coffee.

"Bronc riding's hard work," Edna says sympathetically.

He grins.

"You can't wear the bastard out," he says. "I'll get him though. Soon be tame as a pussycat."

The horsebreaker has been with them three weeks. Stan has taken two broke horses to a horse sale in Lethbridge. It is midnight. The horsebreaker, lying beside her, suddenly bunches his muscles and in one quick movement, turns on his side and gathers her in his arms again.

"I love you," he says into her hair.

"You don't even know me," Edna says. "You just met me."

"What do you stay with him for? Come with me," he says.

"I'm five years older than you are," Edna replies. She is staring at the opposite wall, noticing that the brown stain on the wallpaper near the ceiling is getting bigger. The horsebreaker takes her by the shoulders and pushes her onto her back and kneels above her.

"I'm crazy about you," he whispers, staring into her eyes. His own eyes are like flowers, Edna thinks, cornflowers. There is no depth behind them. He puts his face down into the hollow of her neck and takes her skin gently in his teeth. She is afraid he will leave a mark. He holds her so tightly she can hardly breathe.

"I love you, I love you," he says to her fiercely. "Come with me."

"Maybe," Edna answers looking at the darkness at the edge of the lamp's glow.

Edna is washing dishes. The horsebreaker has gone into town to a movie. It is unusual for Stan to come and sit in the kitchen while she does the supper dishes. He is usually asleep in his chair in front of the TV set by now.

"He's got nothing," Stan says.

16

"Who?" Edna asks. Stan stares at her till she drops her eyes.

"He can't stick to anything, he'll never amount to anything."

"His father didn't leave him a ranch," she says.

"I'm going to throw him out. He's been here a month. The work's done."

"Don't be silly, Stan," Edna says, turning around. "He's nothing to me. I'm not interested in him." She turns back to her dishes.

"I don't like the way he looks at you when he thinks I'm not looking. I wouldn't trust him not to make a pass at you when I'm not around." Edna bangs the frying-pan into the dishwater.

"You wouldn't give a damn," she says. "I'm just something you own, like those horses out there." Stan gets up and goes out of the kitchen.

At breakfast, Stan has told her that the black gelding is still too jumpy, "too goosey," he says. She goes out to watch him work with the horse, knowing what she will see, but unable to stop herself from going. The horse is saddled and standing in the corral. Stan takes another rope, ties it to the side of the saddle and then loops it around the horse's right rear leg. He pulls it tight from the front. The horse tried to free his leg, but Stan is close at his side making the loop into a sling from the side of the saddle around the horse's leg. He loops the rope twice and then secures the end with a couple of half-hitches to the saddle. The horse becomes helpless. He can barely walk on three legs. Then Stan bends carefully at the horse's front legs and hobbles him. Now the horse tries to move and finds himself with only one good leg. He backs into a corner of the corral, supporting his rump against the fence and stands. His front legs begin to shake from the effort of standing in such an unnatural position. Stan takes another rope, secures it to the saddle horn, then throws the loose middle section over the horse's back. Then he walks behind the horse and pulls the rope across his rump. He goes up to the horse and shakes the saddle vigorously. The horse starts to buck and begins to fall. Quickly Stan pulls on the rope and holds him upright. Again he tries to buck, springing upward on his front legs and trying to throw his back legs out. He starts to fall again. Stan pulls him upright again, then snorting, the horse kneels on his front legs and lowers his head to the ground. Stan rubs his back and his flank roughly. The horse leaps upward in a fluid jump that straightens his front legs. Stan walks around him talking to him, patting him, rubbing his head, shaking the saddle, throwing the rope over him. After ten minutes of this, the horse is standing quietly, not flinching at every sound and movement. Stan loosens the ropes, mounts him and rides out of the corral. Edna goes back to the kitchen.

Stan begins to ride all day now too. He tells the horse-breaker not to start another horse, to ride the greenbroke one he worked on first. He himself, Stan says, will ride the big black gelding. So now Edna watches Stan on the black horse ride back and forth in front of her kitchen window all day long. It is much colder now and there is a thin covering of snow on the ground that doesn't melt during the day. At supper the horsebreaker says, "I'll be heading south soon. Winter's coming." Edna doesn't look up from her plate, but her hands are moist and she can feel a flush rising in her cheeks. Stan says heartily, "Be sorry to see you go." He and the horsebreaker talk to one another about Chuck's departure. He says he'll leave Friday. It is Wednesday evening now.

Early Thursday afternoon the horsebreaker corners her in his bedroom where she is making his bed. Stan has just driven off to get the mail, and the horsebreaker has hurried in only bothering to take off his overshoes. He flips his parka hood down and holds her by both arms.

"I'm leaving for Montana. Come with me." His eyes gleam like a coyote's. She thinks, he likes the excitement. He likes the danger. He is so strong that when he pulls her toward him and kisses her, she doesn't even try to resist. She sees herself driving off beside him in his maroon pickup, sees the ranch growing smaller and smaller behind her, sees the road widening, becoming blacktop, leading into a city, its skyscrapers rising mistily toward the morning sun. She imagines the horsebreaker sitting beside her, his heavy thigh touching hers. She begins to kiss him back, raises her arms and puts them around his neck.

"It would be easy," she says, not to him.

"Come," he whispers. "I can't live without you." They hear the purr of Stan's truck driving into the yard. She pulls away and turns to finish making the bed. The horsebreaker hurries into the kitchen where he turns on the tap and takes a glass down from the shelf. In a moment, Stan comes into the house, sets the mail on the table. The horsebreaker wipes his mouth, flips up his parka hood and goes back outside without speaking. Edna finishes and comes back into the kitchen where she sits down at the table across from Stan, who is reading the mail. He lifts his head and studies her, then he goes back to his reading. She looks at Stan a long time, thinking how it used to be when they were first married.

On Friday morning Stan is out at the barn while Chuck is in his bedroom packing. Edna goes to the bedroom door and says to him, "I'm not going with you." He lets his duffel bag fall back on the bed, shirts spilling out of it.

"Please," he says, crossing to her, trying to hold her. "I love you, I can't do without you. Please." He means to overwhelm her with his passion. It makes her angry. She pulls back and hisses, "Can't either of you leave me alone? I'm not a horse that you keep at and keep at until you win." She is furious. Chuck would have slipped to his knees by now if she hadn't jerked away. Suddenly the outer door opens and Stan comes in. Chuck turns back to his packing. Stan stares at Edna as she crosses the room, but she is so angry with both of them that she doesn't falter, and Stan doesn't speak. The horsebreaker takes his duffel bag and walks out without a word. From the sink Edna can see him loading his saddle into his truck. He gets in and drives away.

"Good riddance," Stan says, with more relief than anger in his voice. He puts his arm around her, but she pulls away and faces him.

"What?"

"I'm leaving tomorrow," she says. He drops his arm and stares at her.

"Alone," she says. He tries to make sense of this. She can see his thoughts as they cross his face. Finally, he asks, "When will you be back?" She is silent for a moment. She hadn't thought of coming back, but now she realizes that this is a possibility.

"I don't know," she hesitates.

"Good," Stan says, as if everything is now explained. "A holiday. Go visit Merrilee. You should have gone a long time ago." He doesn't mention her departure again that day. Edna is too baffled by his response, too uncertain of herself to want to talk about this.

In the morning he gives her a cheque for several hundred dollars. Then he says, "Tell Merrilee...good luck." He hands Edna a second cheque and tells her to give it to Merrilee to help pay for moving. "I'll drive you to the bus," he says. "You can use Merrilee's car in the city. Maybe you should go to Vancouver with her. Help her get settled."

He helps her onto the bus, neither of them speaking in front of the ranchers who lounge, gossiping, against their half-tons, or the truckers checking their rigs.

"Phone me," Stan says, holding his hat on against the wind, and turns away. She watches him walk to his truck, climb in and back out without looking at her again. She knows he is afraid to look at her.

Edna sits behind the tinted window glass holding her purse tightly with both hands. It seems thick and clumsy to her, heavy with the weight of the two cheques. As the bus pulls out with a pneumatic sigh, Edna's tears stop as if the source has suddenly dried up. She sits holding her purse, feeling the tight cool tracks that mark her cheeks where her tears had been.

She sits for a long time, for hours, on the bus, watching the passengers sway as if they are one person. It will take more than you and a horsebreaker, she thinks. She sets her purse down on the empty seat beside her and stretches slowly. The bus rolls on west, into the sunset, toward the distant mountains.

O WHAT VENERABLE &
REVEREND CREATURES

"He said it was a heart attack," Meredith said. She could not find the cradle for the phone; the phone wouldn't fit. "He said she was bringing dessert to the table and she started to stagger. She sat down and then she just said, 'oh,' and fell over." Meredith suddenly let go of the receiver and balled the napkin she had been holding, pressing it against her face, trying to stifle the noise she could hear herself making. She heard Bill move, felt his arm go around her, felt his hand smoothing her hair.

"Poor girl," he said. "Poor girl."

There was a rustling in the doorway. Stacey. Stacey would have to be told. Meredith wiped her eyes with the napkin and stood back from Bill who had turned to the door. Stacey was leaning against the door frame, one hand raised to her shoulder, the thin, nicotine-stained fingers twisting a lock of thick, curly brown hair that hung uncombed in a mass around her shoulders. Her eyes glittered. The petulance of her expression made her look younger than eighteen.

"Who was that?" she asked, looking at the phone instead of at them. Even when she was in a rage or coldly withdrawn from them she could not change the startling depth and resonance of her voice. It was the voice of a great stage actress.

"Your Grandpa Robertson," Bill said. "Your grandmother is dead." Meredith put her hand on Bill's arm. These days he was often too harsh with Stacey.

"About two hours ago," she said, and tried to think of something to add that might comfort Stacey. Stacey's expression, held so carefully false for so long, had wavered and almost softened. She took a step into the room, staring at her mother.

"Oh," she said. "Oh." Meredith moved toward Stacey who, remembering herself, stiffened theatrically and made as if to back away.

Bill, watching, his voice impatient, said, "We can get the first flight west in the morning. I'll start making the arrangements." He patted Meredith's shoulder. When he reached the doorway he stopped. "You'd better start packing, Stacey," he said. "You're coming too." Meredith could see the sudden shine of sweat on Stacey's neck as she lifted her chin. They watched her, Bill indifferent, no longer even amused; Meredith sadly, seeing how beautiful she was, like some spoiled decadent rich child in the movies, her rich dark hair, her fine nose, the dark shadows around her eyes, the hysteria always just beneath her skin.

"You must be out of your mind," Stacey said. She shoved

23

her hands into her jeans pockets, lifted her chin and turned toward the door. Bill didn't move, blocking it with his big, square body. He looked down at her. "I can't get away from school," she said. A tremor had crept into her voice as Bill stared at her and didn't move. "You were so damned anxious for me to go back and now..."

"I know it's semester break," Bill interrupted. His voice was tight, his bitterness barely covered. "I know you failed all three courses. The school called my office. They can't see any point in your coming back for another semester. You're just wasting everybody's time, they said." Standing behind her, Meredith saw Stacey's shoulders quiver. Stacey was all quicksand inside and whenever she opened and the wave of her uncertainty pulsed through the air to Meredith, she remembered. Stacey, a four-five-six-year-old, screaming in terror. Smiling in the morning as if there was no blackness, no endless night. "Start packing," Bill said. "We are all going to your grandmother's funeral." Stacey twisted one shoulder and slid past him without speaking.

In the morning they boarded a plane, Bill in his grey three-piece suit, Meredith in her ageing but still smart blue Chanel, and Stacey, rumpled and sleepy, her hair uncombed, wearing fraying faded jeans and a stained brown suede windbreaker. They flew west with Stacey seated several rows behind them stilting their conversation and poisoning Meredith's grief with her hostility, which they could feel boring through the several rows of seats between them.

At Regina they rented a car and drove west for another four hours, soon leaving the wide paved highway for roads that grew narrower and more and more treacherous with snow and ice. Meredith had not been home for more than a year. She was a rancher's daughter, but she had lived the last twenty years in Toronto, and for the last fifteen she had taught chemistry at the university. Each time she returned home she was grateful that she had escaped the hardship, the male chauvinism, the ignorance.

The church was full even though outside a blizzard was blowing. Her father had begun to stoop and to move more slowly. After the service, stepping out of the church onto the snow-covered, windy step, he hesitated and looked around in a bewildered way as if he was surprised to find himself still in the town of his birth.

At the cemetery high on the hillside the wind whipped the snow across the rectangular hole in the ground and made their coats flap against their legs. Stacey had refused to get out of the car although Meredith did not notice this till after. The minister hurried through the ceremony, his words lost in the storm.

The next day Bill left to go back east, leaving Stacey and Meredith behind to look after Meredith's father for a week or two until he "could get back on his feet."

At breakfast when Meredith served him his bacon and eggs, her father put his arm around her and said, "You're a good girl, Merry. Never gave us a moment's trouble. Who'd ever think I'd have a professor for a daughter." Meredith kissed his forehead and sat down. "Your mother and me," he said carefully, as if he was trying out the sound of it, "your mother and me," he repeated, stronger this time, "we..." He seemed to have forgotten what he had started to say.

"Maybe now you'll think about retirement," Meredith said.

"Yeah," he said. He stirred his coffee. "You and Stacey could chase the cows around to the feed ground this morning," he said. "You know, like you used to. It's too damn cold for them to go without feed."

"All right," Meredith said. "It'll be good for Stacey to have something to do."

After her father had gone out, Meredith knocked on

Stacey's door. At home she had given up waking Stacey. Usually she went off to the university and left Stacey in bed. When she came home at night Stacey was usually gone and Meredith would hear her coming in at three or four in the morning deliberately making some noise so that she and Bill would know how late it was.

"Wake up Stacey," she called. "Your grandpa needs us. We have to give him a hand." Silence. "Stacey?" she called, opening the door. Stacey was lying on her back staring at the ceiling. Her clothes were strewn on the floor. The room had a musty, closed-in smell.

Stacey threw back the covers and sat on the side of the bed. Meredith went back to the kitchen. In a few minutes Stacey came in wearing the same jeans and shirt she had worn since the funeral. Her hair needed washing and there was sleep in the corners of her eyes.

"What?" Stacey asked.

"We have to chase the cattle away from the riverbed up onto the feed grounds." Stacey was staring at the outdoor thermometer.

"It's twenty below out there!" she said. "You must be nuts!"

"I am not nuts," Meredith said, banging the coffee-pot. "When it's very cold like this, they go down into all the nooks and crannies along the riverbed looking for shelter." She poured Stacey a cup of coffee without looking at her. "And then they don't hear the tractor, or see the feed coming and they miss it." She put the coffee-pot back on the stove. "And then they can't endure the cold without good feed and they die." She tried to smile at Stacey. "So it is essential that we go out and chase them up. It's only about a mile and a half."

"Christ!" Stacey said, but Meredith saw the welling brightness in her eyes and knew nothing would stop Stacey from going, from trying the bitter air in her lungs, from testing the feel of the thigh-deep snow, from challenging a 1200-pound range cow or as suddenly grovelling in terror in front of one.

On the third morning Stacey rose without being called. She came into the kitchen where Meredith, already wearing most of her outdoor clothes, was hurrying to get the dishes washed before she went out. Stacey poured herself a cup of coffee, not answering her mother's "good morning," and stood watching at the window.

"You don't need to go out this morning," she said. He voice sounded as if she hadn't spoken for weeks. "I know what to do."

"I don't mind," Meredith said.

"I can do it!" Stacey said. "Meredith." She rolled the *r*. Meredith flushed but didn't speak. Stacey put on her parka and went outside. Meredith could hear her whistling for the dogs.

When the dishes were done, the beds made and a pie in the oven, Stacey had still not returned. I'll bet she's romping with the dogs in the snow, or maybe examining those caves along the riverbank, Meredith thought. It surprised her to think that Stacey might be having fun. It struck her now how little fun there was in Stacey's life, or that Stacey, a creature of contradictions, paradoxes and extremes, probably did not know what fun was. Whenever the police brought her back after she had run away (and then seemed not to know what to do with herself, or even why she had gone), she always looked so pale and sickly that Meredith could only pity her, for the demon that pursued her and would not give her peace.

She decided to clean Stacey's room for her as a way of thanking her for saving her from the long, difficult walk along the river bottom. She stripped the bed and put clean sheets on it and put away the discarded clothes. Stacey's suitcase was still lying on the floor. Meredith picked it up by the handle intending to set it upright in the closet, but as she lifted it, it fell open spilling the contents. Oh no, Meredith thought, she'll accuse me of snooping. Quickly she bent over and began to replace the tangled underwear and shirts. Something fell out onto the floor. A plastic bag full of something that looked like dried grass. Meredith picked it up. Marijuana. No wonder the room smelled so stuffy.

I might have known, she thought. Stacey the troublemaker, the eternal embarrassment, the albatross she and Bill wore around their necks. How could she do such a thing? How could she bring this into her grandparents' house, especially at a time like this? She went to the kitchen and looked out the window. Stacey was crossing the yard toward the house, snow clinging to her pants above the knees, the dogs jumping at her side.

She came into the house stamping the snow off her boots, and throwing back her hood. Meredith stood in the doorway of the kitchen facing her, holding the bag chest-high in front of her. Stacey looked at it. For a moment she said nothing. Then she said, "Snooping again?" and grabbed for the bag. Meredith jerked it out of her reach and stepped back into the kitchen.

"How could you do this?" she asked.

"It's only grass, Meredith," Stacey said. "It's no big deal. How could you do this?" she mimicked her mother.

Meredith reached out, she did not know she was going to do this, and slapped Stacey across the face. They stared at each other. Meredith was not sorry she had hit Stacey. Stacey's face had drained white, the red slap mark standing out like a birthmark.

The bag of marijuana had fallen to the floor. Neither of them bent to pick it up. Stacey's eyes began to fill with tears. Two large drops gathered at the bottom of her eye and as Meredith watched, they spilled over and began to run down Stacey's cheeks.

"You have caused me so much pain," Meredith said. She bent and picked up the bag, took it to the half-bath that was by the backdoor, emptied it into the toilet and flushed it. Stacey still had not moved. Meredith had begun to shake. She waited for the screams, the attack, or the fainting.

There was a thumping on the step outside the door and then Meredith's father called, opening the door, "Somebody give me a hand here." Meredith opened the door. He was struggling into the house pushing a slick, reddish creature ahead of him. Stacey gasped and put her hand over her mouth.

"It's a new calf, sweetheart," her grandfather said, laughing at her expression. If he saw the red mark or the tears, he gave no sign.

"Is it alive?" Stacey asked. "Ugh!" she said. "It's all slimy!" Her grandfather put the calf down on the hall floor with a thump.

"Got to get it warmed up," he said, "or it'll die."

"What are you doing, Dad, calving in January?" Meredith asked. She was surprised at how normal her voice sounded.

"Goddamn bulls must have got in with the heifers last spring. I found this one near the feed grounds, just born."

"Heifer okay?" Meredith asked, falling into the language.

"Yeah, that one's all right, but I found another dead one north. Calving too long. I didn't know they'd been bred. You can't tell with heifers. Now look at the mess. It's ears are frozen down."

"The cord's frozen too," Meredith said. Behind her, Stacey made a "yuck" sound. Meredith was surprised Stacey was still there.

"It'll be safe in the half-bath till it gets warm and dries

off," he said. "I didn't dare leave it for the mother to lick it off." He stood up. "There's bound to be more," he said. "I have to go check the rest of the herd. Keep on eye on it, Merry," he said. "You too, Stacey." He went outside. Stacey knelt, ignoring Meredith, cooing to the calf.

In the late afternoon Meredith's father came back to the house carrying another calf. Meredith was reading in the living-room. When she went to the kitchen she saw Stacey on her hands and knees in the half-bath trying to dry the calf off with Meredith's blow-dryer. Her grandfather was kneeling beside her, talking to her. Meredith left the room quickly before either of them saw her.

Every morning Stacey chased the cattle down the riverbed and when she finished that, she went up to the feed grounds and helped her grandfather and his hired man fork the hay off the flatdeck to the waiting cattle. After that the three of them would come in for the noon meal that Meredith would have ready and then, leaving the dishes for Meredith, they would go down to the barn and help the new calves nurse. Stacey usually didn't answer if Meredith spoke to her. The days dragged by.

Meredith's father came hurrying in late one afternoon.

"Jim and I have to take that steer to the vet," he said. "We should be back by seven. Got a heifer due to calve in the barn so I have to get back as soon as I can."

Stacey ate her supper in front of the television set in the living-room. Meredith ate at her place in the kitchen.

At eight o'clock Meredith's father had still not returned. The temperature had dropped to thirty below and the wind was rising. She supposed he was storm-stayed somewhere. After a lifetime in this country, she told herself, he will know how to take care of himself. Remembering the heifer, she put on her parka and went down to the barn. It had begun to calve. She could see the end of one tiny hoof protruding from beneath the upraised tail. She studied the

30

heifer nervously. She couldn't tell if it had been trying to deliver for a long time or not. Oh lord, she thought, what will I do? She decided to wait an hour before she tried to help. Maybe her father would be back by then.

At nine o'clock she went back to the barn. Now she could see both hooves. That's too slow, she said to herself. I'm pretty sure that's too slow. We'll have to help her. I wish Dad would get home. She went back to the house and said, "Stacey," to her daughter who had not taken her eyes off the television.

"What?" Stacey said.

"That heifer can't deliver on her own, and your grandfather's not back and...we'll have to pull it."

"Pull it yourself," Stacey said.

"I can't, Stacey," Meredith cried. "I'm not strong enough. You have to help me. I can't do it alone." To her amazement tears were running down her cheeks. She wiped them off and then stared at the wet streak on her hand. Stacey was watching her now, that brightness back in her eyes. "Please help me, Stacey," she said. "The heifer will die if we don't pull her calf. And the calf will die right away if we don't get it out of there." Stacey's eyes, wide, bright and hard, had shifted away from Meredith to some invisible thing; her mouth was open, she was almost smiling. She rose and went to the kitchen with Meredith following and put on her borrowed parka, her boots and mittens.

The weather had been getting steadily worse. When they opened the back door it blew out of their hands and banged against the wall. They had to walk backwards to the barn, the wind, bitterly cold now, was blowing into their faces with such force.

"Well, where is she?" Stacey asked when they were inside the barn. Meredith pointed. The cow raised her head and mooed. Stacey went to her and stared at the little pair of

31

hooves. "How do we pull it?" she asked.

"This is all I know how to do," Meredith said. She picked a rope hanging from a nail on the wall. It had a loop on one end. She went to the heifer and set the loop over the two protruding hooves and tightened it. "Take the end." She held onto the rope just ahead of Stacey. "Pull!" Meredith grunted. "One, two, three!" They pulled so hard that when the calf came in one whoosh, they fell backward into the straw on top of each other.

"We did it!" Stacey said, standing and staring at the calf.

"I bet it weighs close to a hundred pounds," Meredith said. They took the rope off the calf and stood back, their white breaths fading above them.

"I don't know how we're going to get it to the house, especially in that wind."

"It'll freeze to death if we don't," Stacey said. She pushed open the barn door. They each took an end of the calf and staggering with its weight, floundering in the snowdrifts, falling, being pushed off course and blinded by the wind-driven snow, they got the calf to the house. It had taken them fifteen minutes. They put the calf in the half-bath and Meredith turned up the thermostat.

"It looks okay," Stacey said dubiously.

"Well, it doesn't look any worse than the others did anyway," Meredith answered. "I'll put some coffee on. I hope Dad gets here soon."

They turned the television set on and sat drinking coffee in the warm living-room. Now and then the calf in the bathroom bleated and made a knocking noise with its hooves as it tried to stand.

"I can just imagine the mess in there," Meredith said. Stacey laughed. "I wish we'd had time to spread news-papers." Suddenly she realized that she had not been watching Stacey, she had been only looking at her as one person looks at another during a conversation. It had been years,

years, since she had simply talked to Stacey, since she had been able to forget that this was her disturbed, delinquent child who couldn't be trusted, who had to be watched. Now she noticed that Stacey had put on a little weight, she was not quite so painfully, deliberately thin, and her skin was less yellowish and sickly looking. Stacey had lit a cigarette and was lounging in the chair laughing at something on the television. Her socks were not clean. Her jeans were worn out and clumsily patched, her cotton shirt faded and she wore no bra under it.

Meredith had a sense of the shadows around the edges of the room darkening, of Stacey's form taking on a depth, a richness of colour, another dimension that made her more real, like the central figure in a Rembrandt.

Do I really love her, Meredith asked herself? She remembered what the school psychologist had said when Stacey was fourteen and had been caught in the boys' bathroom with five or six boys.

"I think, Mrs. Gilchrist, that some kids are already lost." Her hair was greying. She would soon retire. "I've been at this work a long time. I know I shouldn't say this to you. But I think some kids are lost. I mean from the moment they breathe on their own. I don't know why it should be that way." She had looked very old. Meredith could hardly believe that this was the same woman who stood up at community meetings and gave speeches on "You and your teenager." "Take her to a psychiatrist." That was all she had said.

When Meredith had asked the psychiatrist for some word, for some explanation, he had said only, "No-one is responsible for what Ortega called, 'this terrible reality.'" Meredith did not know what he meant.

Do I really love her, she asked herself again?

She had been an ordinary baby, her brown eyes alert and intelligent, quick to smile, and when she could walk, she had been into everything like all babies. She was slightly underweight at birth, she cried too much, Meredith had worked all through her childhood, but none of these things, not together, not singly, accounted for Stacey. Nothing accounted for Stacey. She would be their burden all the rest of their lives.

They stayed up to watch the late movie and during it both Stacey and Meredith fell asleep. The next time Meredith looked at her watch it was six o'clock. Her father, still wearing his snowmobile suit, was looking down at her.

"Had to sleep in the truck till it cleared," he said. He sat down heavily in a chair and unzipped his suit. "I'm getting too old for this," he said. "I'm going to have to cut back on my herd come spring. I don't know how I'd have managed without you two this last couple of weeks."

He had grown older since her last visit. He was an old man. He couldn't be left alone. She was his only relative, the only one left to manage the burden of his life. It would be impossible for him to live in the city. In the city, living with them, he would die. She should stay here and look after him. He had leaned back. His eyes were closed and sadness wrapped around him like a cloak. I should stay, she thought. Snow was banked up around the picture window and the stars were still out.

"Yes, you'll have to cut back," she said. "I hate to leave you, Dad, but I have to get back to my job, to Bill."

"I know, I know," her father said. He looked across to the window as if to hide his despair from her. One way or another, she thought, our children all break our hearts. It is the way things are.

Stacey, lying on the couch near them, stirred and they both turned to her. She sat up and they saw that she had been awake through their talk. Her expression was open, her voice heartbreakingly beautiful.

"I'm staying," she said. Meredith and her father looked at her. Meredith opened her mouth to speak. "It's my life," Stacey said to her. She looked back to her grandfather. "I'm staying," she said.

Meredith's father drove her to town where she caught a bus to Regina, and from Regina, a plane to Toronto. It was a flight that had originated in Vancouver and the plane was full. A young mother and her four-year-old boy sat beside Meredith, the mother at the window, the child in the middle and Meredith on the aisle. The child was active, sitting on his mother's knee at the window, asking for water, asking to go to the bathroom, whining for a toy.

"I don't know what to do with him," the young woman said to Meredith, apologetically. Meredith thought, I could tell her that he's not bothering me, or that he will probably grow up to be Prime Minister, or at least a decent, normal adult. Or I could tell her that there will come a time when she will wonder whether she loves him. There will come a time when you will both have to realize that it is his life, that he will have to find his own way in the world, that he will be what he is.

Instead, she said, "He's a handsome child, and he seems quite bright." After a while she said, "I have a daughter, she's grown up now. She was a beautiful baby, lots of dark hair and big brown eyes, and always asking questions too. She used to love to throw bread to the pigeons in the park. She wasn't at all afraid of them. They would come closer and closer and she would stand still, her little arm outstretched with the bread in her hand. They would take it out of her fingers and how that delighted her. Once, one perched on her shoulder and she smiled, there was such wonder in her smile and in her eyes."

But the little boy was squirming again, he had climbed from his seat and was banging on the window with a toy car. His mother held his arm to stop him and he began to wail. The young woman was not listening to Meredith. But Meredith hardly noticed. She leaned back in her seat and closed her eyes. All the way home she thought about Stacey in the park with the pigeons.

THE MISSION

My husband once threw all my paintings in the Halifax dump. He did it only once. I never painted again and since I eventually divorced him anyway, he never had the opportunity to do it a second time. I imagine him, while I am sleeping peacefully upstairs in the master bedroom beside my second or third husband, sneaking in down below and quietly slipping each of my paintings off its hook in the living-room and the dining-room, even the one that hangs in the hall that I thought he would never notice, moving slowly sideways out the patio door, holding them carefully in his black-gloved hands, and loading them one by one into his Volkswagen and stealing away in the night. I can see the corners of the pictures—they are all still-lifes of fruit and flowers, sticking out the window of the car, before they disappear into the darkness, as he makes his way to the dump with them. Perhaps this time it is Vancouver or Yellowknife or the outskirts of a village in Spain. Will I never be safe from him?

After the divorce, a friend of mine who is a poet used to say this would make a great short story, and although I have never been able to figure out how, I have decided to try. The thing is, do I make it up? Do I tell it as it really happened? Do I remember how it happened? I know we were moving. From one apartment to another. He drove to the dump, opened the trunk of the car (an American Motors Rambler, pale blue), and pitched them, one by one, frames and all, onto the rat-infested junk heap.

I married again. A nice man. Very quiet. A farmer. We live in the country on the outskirts of a medium-sized prairie city and all my friends are other farmers' wives. Our conversations are about gardening and raising children and whether Debbie Pankowski was pregnant at her wedding or not. This morning my nearest neighbour, Cheryl, mother of three, came over for coffee and caught me at my typewriter.

"Just writing a letter for Wayne," I said quickly.

"Didn't know you could type," she said, looking around the room with a suspicious air, holding Melinda, her three-year-old between her knees while Melinda struggled to get free. Is this going to be one of those boring women's stories? I hope not. I pulled the sheet of paper, this sheet, out of the typewriter and put it casually face down on the counter out of her reach while I made the coffee.

"I write a lot of Art's letters for him, too," she said. She is afraid that I am better educated than she is.

"What would they do without us?" I asked. She laughed.

38

"Find another sucker, I guess," she said.

Actually I have no friends in the country. Just women who are suspicious of me and who dislike me but are curious about me and my probably disreputable past. How do they sense this? Can they smell it on my clothes? Is it etched in the lines on my face? For my part I try to be nice although vague, but I find this hard to maintain. Leon spoiled me for all that. He showed me too clearly what hypocrites we all are, and how there is very little good in the human heart, if any. So I shouldn't have been surprised or hurt when he threw all my paintings in the Halifax dump.

Why were we in Halifax moving from apartment to apartment? Me pained and apologetic, Leon reckless and pleased by the abandonment of emptied rooms, surprised by each forgotten box of blankets or books, each broken dish, each lost neighbour, eager for unfamiliar sets of stairs and a landlord's quirks.

I forget why. He didn't like his job, he changed courses at the university, or he found this place or that unbearable because at one the landlord's wife played tunes he hated on her piano, or at another, the rooms were too clean, had no quaint nooks, or the neighbours too middle-class, too cautious, saved their money and wore overcoats in winter and pigskin gloves with whip-stitching on the seams.

I can smell the sea. Seagulls wheel and scream. I find a scalpin on the beach. A man in blue trunks wearing a face mask is diving from a yellow rubber dinghy out at the edge of the bay. He has a spear in his hand. I grow more despondent as I write.

I was working for a private agency as a teacher-social worker with teenaged boys who had been thrown out of school or dropped out or had possibly never gone, had no jobs and didn't want any and were drunks or glue-sniffers or both, or bootleggers, or were fresh out of jail or waiting

39

trial to go in, or out on day parole from the city jail.

I met them each day in a mission in the north end. The dilapidated wooden building ran storey by storey up the side of the city, its back windows overlooking the harbour and the rats and ships, its front walls blank to the long double row of blacks that snaked up the sidewalk every Tuesday morning when the mission passed out free clothing and coupons for groceries. "Let the lady past, let the lady past." Elaborate courtesy to a little white girl in her nice brown wool coat with the fur collar trying to get into the building early. I dared to try to teach their own, to try to resurrect them when they could not, when they viewed their own miscreants with hatred born of their own failure and helplessness; backing away too far with exaggerated outspread arms, "Let the lady past," like voices in a nightmare, the very fur of my collar wilting under their sarcastic grovelling.

Leon worked or didn't work, went to school or didn't go to school. Got drunk, slept with best friends' sisters, stayed up all night reading, threw paintings in the dump.

And I taught the boys. Each day they came to torment me with their bitterness, their hatred-blunted intelligence, their frightened love, and each day I set out to win them all with jokes, with smiles, with tears, nothing was beneath me. Their faces gleam at me brown, mauve-tinted, like no colour anywhere else on earth, so beautiful that I would stare and think: how would you paint that? What colours in my tubes of paint would blend to make that gleaming swelling of cheek, that blackness under the eyes in delicate folds of satin flesh, that glow that is not so much brown or black as living, shimmering earth colours highlighted by sunlight: brass and copper?

I will not talk about painting. I don't do that anymore. Don't think I had any talent anyway.

Above the fridge the clock ticked and the coffee-pot

sighed now and then on the stove. Cheryl was sipping her second cup of coffee while Melinda sat in the middle of the yellow-tiled kitchen floor and chewed on the pages of a magazine her mother had given her to keep her quiet. I stirred my coffee and listened to the birds chirping in the poplars outside the kitchen. The inside back door and the window above the sink were open. A spring breeze stirred the white organdie curtains.

"I'm going to get my garden in this week," Cheryl said. "The weather report sounds good. Art is going to plough it up after supper tonight."

"Did your order come from the seed company?" I asked her.

"Yeah, yesterday," Cheryl said. Melinda got to her knees and stood up. She toddled to the back door and stood with her nose pressed to the screen watching my white housecat sunning himself on the back step. If I listened carefully between breaths, every once in a while I could hear Wayne's tractor as it came to the end of the field nearest the house and then slowly retreated.

"Time to get dinner on," Cheryl said. She's much younger than I am, but already she is losing that slimness through the waist and there are wrinkles developing in the corners of her eyes. I suppose under her clean cotton blouse her breasts are beginning to sag. I smiled and waved once as she drove away.

When was he good to me? When did he love me? I want to write that part here, to slide in a poignant interlude of peace and beauty, to help you see why we were there together. But my mind has shut that part off, blanked it out, erased it, buried it, blotted it out, thrown it in the dump with the paintings. I concentrate but nothing comes. But wait: we travelled together most of the way across Canada, 3000 miles, to find the Maritimes we knew from small indistinct black and white photos in the corners

of the pages of our history texts, the Maritimes of fisher-
men lifting torn nets, smoking pipes and wearing suspen-
ders and black rubber boots too large for them, of haunted
lighthouses and Atlantic storms and apple orchards. In our
Volkswagen piled high with books and curtains and
frying-pans and (I hate to say this, I really do) diapers.
Diapers. And a baby. Let us not forget there was a baby. A
chubby boy with intelligent eyes and a chin like his
father's. Picture me stopping in the blue Rambler in front
of the nursery each day, carrying the baby in, running out
again and driving off in the rain.

The boys sit around a long table. The door at the far end
of the narrow room opens and all our heads swivel to see
who will come in. It is Tuesday, mission day. The building
is busy, full of nice white ladies scurrying around the hall
below the church folding worn dresses, sweaters with missing buttons, old-fashioned pants with wide legs and cuffs,
mismatched boots. How do the poor accept these things? I
never stop to watch, I scurry past the rows of rickety tables,
head down, up the stairs, shut the door behind me, big
flakes of wet snow vanishing on my coat and boots.

Ah, but its Billy Gregg, big Billy Gregg, just out of jail
yesterday. All around the table breath is held, faces freeze,
fingers stop moving. In prison he worked out every day and
married a white girl who came to the jail for the wedding.
He is so big it is said the police are afraid of him. He looks
around the room, we're at the very top of the building, the
roof slants downward over our heads, the dark-stained
cupboards are kept locked, the choir gowns hang blood-
red out of our reach. It is too stuffy, it is damp in here.

A student sleeps without a sound in the leather chair
with the sagging bottom pushed against the wall by my
desk that sits crossways in the corner. I lean back against
the desk, holding a textbook against my breasts with one
arm, fussing with my hair with the other hand. I am

wearing my green checked dress with the red trim around the wrists. The boys watch to see what I will do when I see who has stepped inside the room, his face held in a grin, he is sidling between the backs of their chairs and the dirty plaster wall toward me. There is no sound in the room but the swish of his clothes, the quickness of his breath.

I lower the book slowly without realizing it until I am holding it loosely in my hand, waist-high. He is in front of me now, the size of a bulldozer, an apartment-building, a heavy-weight boxer. I stare up at him, horrified, the blood has left my head. Am I going to faint? He puts his hands on my arms above the elbows, beside my breasts. My mouth opens. I gasp.

This is not a dream. I will not wake up. Oh, no, I think, oh, no. But suddenly, still holding my arms, his grin vanishes, his face greys, a frightened look appears in his eyes. He drops his hands. He back out of the room.

"I didn't mean nothin'," he says. And the door shuts behind him. What has happened here? Nothing that hasn't happened before, although never before to me. Black man confronts white woman. Black man backs down. White woman is left dizzy with fear and guilt.

I get home in time to cook supper. Our boy, yes, is still there, playing on the rug in front of the television set. *Get Smart* is on. Black and white. Leon comes in from somewhere and picks up our child and together they watch TV while I cook in the kitchenette and set the table. I am still wearing my green-checked dress. I try not to burn anything or cut myself when I peel the vegetables although my hands are still shaking. I stir the pudding and listen for the news to come on. Our boy is giggling. He loves *Get Smart*. Leon laughs too. The pudding is ready. The vegetables are cooked. The sausages are crisp.

Sometimes a student stops coming and I go out on the streets to find him. This house is flush with the sidewalk.

It is painted wine, a dead shade without resonance. The door is made of vertical slabs and instead of a doorknob it has a latch on it like a gardening shed. For a long time nobody answers my knock: what kind of trouble is this? Finally, Travis, the boy I am looking for, opens the door. I step inside, downward.

The floor is dirt. Flattened cardboard boxes have been spread over it. There seem to be no windows. Outside, the traffic whizzes by six feet away. His mother is short, not so much fat as heavy-set, thick, like a man. She is wearing a print dress and stands with her back against the table edge and her hands spread out on it. Nobody asks me to sit down. In the next room, dusky, cave-like, I can see the TV on and hear its murmur although I am too far away to see what the show is or to make sense out of any of the noises.

Soon the other son, Brian, comes into the kitchen from the living-room. There is something passive, blank, about him. He listens but appears not to hear. He looks as if my hand would go right through him if I touched him. He has just come home from two years in Dorchester Penitentiary and he is still not sure where he is.

Wayne and I often go to dances. Last weekend the hall was packed. I caught only glimpses of the bride's white-veiled head now and then as I was pushed around the dance floor by sweating farmers in white shirts and baggy dark suit-pants. It was much too hot, there were too many people packed into the hall and the men had opened all the doors. through them, between the heads of the dancers, I could see the indigo night, the faint sprinkling of stars blotted out by the flash of headlights, someone coming or going. The violin, the piano, the thump of the bass guitar drifted outward through the doors and tinkled into the blackness.

"How's seeding going?" my partners asked over and over again. "Wayne got an air seeder yet?" One, two, three, one, two, three. My turquoise skirt ballooned out behind me and then swished back against my legs, my breath coming quickly. I could hear the blood whispering to me in my ears.

"Good dance," Wayne said on the way home. I looked over at him. The moonlight shone in the window and lit up his shoulder and hands on the steering-wheel. His outline was soft, blurred. I looked down at my hands and in the moonlight I could see the loose skin wrinkled, waffled in a way that only happens to women who are into middle-age. My hands seemed pathetic to me, small, ageing, lost.

Down below on my right the harbour stretches out in the sun, cobalt blue with white and cadmium yellow highlights. Tugs chug past, one going this way, one going that. The ferry cuts a diagonal swath through the ships. I have learned to tell the oil tankers from the other cargo ships. On my left the cars rush past, I can hardly hear myself think for the noise. The boys and I have just left the police station where the court was held. They have dispersed in different directions and I am going back to my classroom. I am thinking about how his face paled suddenly as if he were having a heart attack or a stroke, a sudden draining; his shock, disbelief, hitting us like a breaker washing to the back of the court where we are sitting on the wooden benches. Two years. The boys on each side of me fall like dominoes. We all know they will be next. I begin to cry.

Someone is riding a bike beside me. I turn to look. I am not crying anymore. The boy is very tall, so tall that his long gaunt legs look ludicrous on the child's bike he is half-riding, half-pushing along with his feet on the sidewalk. We are on a street lifted high above the harbour—the clock on Citadel Hill above us on our left is silent. He is wearing a long, stained, beige trenchcoat. It is hanging open and the corners of the skirt drag on the sidewalk. His hair has

45

been shaved down to his skull. His skin is more yellow than black and he is very thin. The bones of his face stand out making clear planes, triangles, rectangles of yellow or brown. I think: burnt sienna, yellow ochre, titanium white.

"Hey, Mrs. Jones, you gonna buy me some socks? I ain't got no socks. I'm too poor to buy socks." Involuntarily I look down at his ankles. He is wearing greying tennis shoes with holes in them. He has no socks on, and his ankles remind me of statues of Christ hanging on the cross that I used to see at mass when I was a child. Christ's were smooth, elegant, graceful. His are bony, angular, ugly. I imagine myself adding just a touch, a flicker of violet in the shadow under the ankle bone.

I don't answer, only smile. There is 50¢ in my purse. We are almost back at the mission. I begin to run, hurrying through the side door, pound up the stairs to the high, small room the church ladies assigned to me when they decided to carpet the large room we had at first, so they could drink their tea in comfort.

I shut the door behind me. The building is very quiet. Somewhere in one of the labyrinthine dirty rooms with the dark varnished walls, the minister is praying. The secretary is typing somewhere else. In one of the rooms in the basement a man is lifting weights, sweating, breathing, waiting. I sit down at my desk.

The door opens, the boy comes in. He is eighteen, nineteen, he has grown larger in the last few minutes. He is wider and the coat he is wearing flaps against the backs of the chairs as he comes toward me down the narrow room. His eyes, yellow-black, look through me, beyond me, past me, perhaps he doesn't know I am here.

"You gonna let me into your class?" he wheedles. He comes closer. "I wanna learn something too...I'm some uneducated...I ain't never gone to school...." His voice is rising, it is a whine, someone else's voice. His words mean nothing to either of us, he could be reciting the Koran or the names of the streets in Khatmandu...he is almost on me. I scream.

"Get out! Get out! Get out!" He pauses, hesitates, I keep screaming, he drops his hands, turns and leaves. My voice is louder than his, he gives up. The minister comes running up the stairs, passes the boy. When I have calmed down, he tells me that I am the wrong person for the job, that I can't do it and that I should accept this. He leaves me sitting at my desk. An hour passes and then I go downstairs and find the boy, who is in one of the basement rooms throwing baskets. I apologize. When I come back upstairs the minister tells me he was wrong, he sees that I was able to face my feelings and deal with them.

"Jesus Christ!" Leon says. "Will you make up your mind? Do you want to go to a movie or to the bar?" He is furious. He has stopped the pale blue Rambler in the middle of the traffic and won't move it until I answer him. In the light from the neon signs his silhouette is sharp as knives, he looks satanic as he glares at me.

"I don't...I don't know," I whimper. Hidden in the sleeves of my coat my hands are trembling again. "I don't know!" I shout, and begin to cry. He makes a disgusted noise and turns back to the traffic. "A movie, a movie," I say quickly. "A movie."

"Which one?" he yells. It is raining, a light rain, but cold. The sky is black above the buildings. The streets are too narrow and the traffic is heavy; it hisses past us on each side. Through the streaked window I see the blurred ultramarine and carmine of the movie houses' and night-clubs' signs. The people are lined up neatly, quietly, under their umbrellas, waiting. Their faces are pale smears, their clothes dark, shapeless in the rain.

47

Now this is the part I have lost, or thrown away. When we get home after the movie he makes love to me. But how? What was it like? Was it fast or slow? That long smooth sarabande that lovers dance between the sheets in the half-light, bodies liquid, sweetly touching, breathing one another's breath, whispering, sighing—there is only an empty space where that part should be. Like an empty white wall after a painting has been stolen.

Wayne and I watch TV at night. He likes cop shows. I don't care what we watch. I sit beside him on the couch leaning against him. He rests one heavy, muscled arm around my shoulders. The lamp is on, and the television is the only voice for a mile in each direction in the prairie night, the darkness. Night after night I fall asleep feeling the warmth of his chest on my ear and cheek, his breath stirring my hair. The stars shine in the window when we go to bed and light his face on the pillow.

Leon and I always go to the monthly shows at the Nova Scotia College of Art gallery. We walk around, he says nothing, I don't speak either. When he asks I say only, "I like this one, this one bores me." The show is from Saskatchewan. We straggle in the door, Leon picking up a program for himself. I pause to wait for him and when I turn for the first quick glance around the hall, I see space, the sky rises above me, the walls recede, I can feel the wind blowing through the room, distance, vastness, home.

Occasionally when Wayne and I drive to town or to a neighbour's for supper, the light strikes the long white grass in such a way, or pours bronze across a field of wheat, or in the fall I see the not-quite-black and rust and olive of the weeds beside a dugout and I know for an instant how to paint it. I blink and look away.

Tick does not want to learn to read he says. I sit beside him on the wooden chair. We are alone at the long oak table. The others have gone, their excuses made one by one:

"My aunt died last night. I have to buy her a dress to be buried in."

"My old man threw me out last night. I have to see my probation officer, find a place to stay."

"I think the cops are looking for me. This is where they'll come. I gotta go."

"The cops beat me up last night all about the head and chest." (He has a black eye.) "I gotta get some sleep."

Tick has stopped reading. The room is quiet. He has closed his eyes, pretends to sleep. His feet are up on the chair across from him. I pull the chair out from under his feet. They fall with a crash on the wooden floor. He starts to read again, stumbling and pausing.

"I ain't readin' no more," he says, shutting the book and folding his arms across his chest.

"Yes, you are, you dope!" I yell. I hit him on the shoulder with the book and open it again. He reads some more. When he can't get a word his large hands holding the book tremble.

"Good, good," I keep saying. "That's good." Sometimes he throws the book across the room, or curses in a joyful way and I laugh.

Now I remember. Not for long, only one flash, flaring up to light the past, then fading into darkness. His touch on me, on my face in the night.

Wayne turns over.

"Are you crying?" he asks in a surprised voice.

"No, no," I say. "I was only yawning and my eyes watered." He turns over again and goes back to sleep.

In the morning Wayne goes out to the field to work. I stand on the back steps. It is almost summer. The crop is up. Beyond the yard and its border of steel grain bins, the now empty barn, the clothesline, the crop rises in a slow curve toward the edge of the earth, toward the sky. They tell me you can't see the harbour from that street anymore. New buildings, offices, hotels, restaurants with ferns and ivy in the window block the view. The mission has been torn down.

The first field is green and just beyond it, if I stand very still and squint, I can make out the huge red and yellow tractor leaving behind it a long swath of black in the fading stubble. I can't hear it, although I hold my breath and listen. Above us, the sky lifts endlessly. I imagine Wayne inside the cab turning his head and looking across the fields, trying to see me, but no matter how hard he strains, he cannot see me in the distance.

BONNIE BURNARD

GRIZZLY MOUNTAIN

She was to leave on Monday. He would help her pack, would carry her bag down to the hotel, would load her into the station-wagon that carried people into the city. He would close the door on her and her bag so that sound would be the sound of ending. He said it was right that she should go through the physical act of removing herself from him. He said it would help if she could put a distance between them, said it was healthy. He had already put his distance there.

And he said they might as well go on the climb as planned, as promised. The exertion would be a cleansing. She allowed him these pronouncements because she knew

52

she would think of him for a long time and it would be useful to think of him sometimes as a pompous ass.

They had lived in this tiny mountain town for three years. It was a poor town but so isolated that those who lived there were allowed to forget their poverty most of the time. The people had no apparent past, talked not about themselves as they sat in the hotel beer-parlour but about the ones who had left when the mine shut down years before and about the ones who had drifted in and out of town since. He was here to teach their kids; she was here to be with him.

They had climbed the mountain before, in the winter. They'd had cross-country skis and good boots to change into when they had to leave the skis behind at the base of the mountain. It had been better between them then. She remembered that he smiled whenever he looked at her on that climb, remembered how his face would seem to take the smile from her, would hold it after he turned away. It made her feel very strong and beautiful. Now that he didn't find his smiles in her she felt, sometimes, repulsive.

The boy had been promised the climb. He was a student, a small tight boy with beige hair and beige skin and eyes as blue as the lakes that could be seen from the top of the mountain, after the climb. And he had shadows drifting across his eyes, like the clouds drifting in reflection across the lakes.

The boy worshipped the man. It was good clean worship, full of imitation and quick grins. The boy's father had been one of the men who had left the town years before. He had neither returned nor sent for his family. The boy didn't speak of his absent father and she suspected it was because he had learned, quite bravely, to live with the unspeakable. She often thought when she looked at the boy that she could kill a man who left a child. A man who could turn his back on that kind of love had nothing to do with life. A man like that was an aberration.

It took no particular effort to include the boy in their lives; he was just quietly there with them, leaving at night to go to his own bed as a child of their own might have done. He hadn't been told that she was leaving. He would know on Monday. She thought maybe her leaving would clear some space for him around the man, maybe even please him. There was certainly no need to exclude him from this last climb. Nothing profound would be said. She knew the danger of trying to say things for the sake of memory. There would be no closing ceremony. They were stopping in the middle, not the end.

They packed the gear the night before the climb, packed the food in the morning, after breakfast. They would have cheese and salami and molasses bread for lunch, cold chicken later in the evening, at the fire. And wine, though it made her sneeze. It was one of the things that got under his skin, her sneezing. They often took wine with them on small hikes out to one of the lakes where they could be alone, where they could claim all the space around them, miles of it. He needed that much space and he loved the wine then. The sneezing had overtaken her on one of their first hikes and he'd looked aghast, said it was like farting in a cathedral. She had laughed. She had no particular respect for cathedrals. In retrospect, she began to recognize the comment as a sign that there would be things about her that he would not forgive.

But he was a good friend to her in their bed and on the mountain wildflowers and on the stony beaches. He had said she was the space he needed, she was distance, said he could be in her without being aware of her breathing on him. She didn't care about the defining of it, only hoped she could always be distance, if that was what he loved.

When it was time to set out in the morning, the boy was at the door with his packsack, ready. He offered no hints of manhood. He was graceful and confident, had not yet begun to stretch and stumble. She had seen him swim nude many times and he was hairless, his skin innocent and fresh in the sun. And he took her own nudity with just a slight puzzlement. She was confident she did not exist in his dreams.

He helped her fasten her packsack, gave the man a fake punch on the shoulder and they started out away from the town. When they were nearly at the end of Main Street the man who ran the coffee shop waved and hailed them, quickly put a half-dozen warm cinnamon buns in a bag and gave it to them, as he had done on other mornings. He had been a friend of the boy's father, years ago.

They didn't talk as they walked, even the boy didn't need talk. They went with silent determination into the space, the distance. It would not have seemed like space to her at all a few years before. Space was uninterrupted, immeasurable distance, space was snow blankets tucked tight across the prairie, the mildest curve of hills almost immodest. This space was unsettled, flamboyant. The land seemed actually to move as you watched it. It climbed uncontrolled toward the clouds, climbed till it was clear of the trees, threw itself over the top of mountains, eager for valleys. It split itself into streams at their feet, gathered together again to hold arrangements of wild flowers and scrub.

The boy sometimes went on ahead of them, blazing a new trail with the small hatchet the man had given him for his eighth birthday. Sometimes he strayed behind them. She sensed he did this so he could have them framed against the dark growth through which they were climbing, as in a picture. Occasionally he would hustle up to her if there were rocks to manage or a stream to jump across, would take her hand in his small one, like an escort.

They were two hours reaching the top of the mountain

and they were greeted by deer scrambling over the far edge, giving up their territory, as they always did. The deer would be back, though they would not come close.

The three of them set up camp together, established a place for the fire, put their sleeping-bags out, three in a row, gathered twigs and dead grass. They would go back down the side later, collect dead wood for the fire. She broke open the food pack, started to slice cheese and meat with the fine cool blade of the hunting-knife, which the man carried in its sheath on his belt. He'd bought the knife as a present for himself with his first paycheque three years ago. He'd come back from shopping with the knife and a shawl for her. The shawl was creamy white with mauve and blue threads woven into the edging. He'd wrapped it around her and slipped the knife over his belt and they sat together quietly in front of the fire.

He had been right about the exercise of the climb. She had forgotten for all that time that she would be leaving on Monday. Here, at the top of the mountain, eating bread and cheese and meat, she remembered. She thought that if the boy hadn't come, if they had been alone, she might have tried to create a final afternoon. But such a final afternoon would have held chaotic words like sorry and maybe and impossibility. Such a final afternoon would have been like this landscape. She held herself flat and silent, allowed no movement, no shadows. It took all of her energy to keep the calm in force.

The man and the boy played chase. They ran over to the tiny lake near the far edge, threw themselves on the grass, rolling over and over, yelling and laughing, uninhibited, free of all restraint but gravity. She knew they would, if not for that one unavoidable pull, without any hesitation, leap off the mountain.

They returned to her and they all slept for a while, together in their row of sleeping-bags and when they awoke the deer were back, grazing. The deer stayed this time and the boy began to talk. He talked of an uncle who had a farm in the south of the province and of another who had a fishing-boat. They moved from those uncles to others, the boy anxious to be told of other kinds of people, other kinds of towns and landscapes. They took him across the prairies and up across the shield, around Lake Superior and down into the south where so many people lived, and through Quebec, through maple sugar bushes and small farms, on through the eastern provinces where they tried to imitate for him the way the people talked and he laughed hard at their effort, threw his head back and held his stomach and she wanted to hug him tight. They took him to that other coast with its steep cliffs and its deadly ocean.

And the man took him to England while she prepared their supper, divided the chicken among them. The boy very quietly, without taking his eyes off the man, got a bag out of his pack. In the bag were three chocolate bars and a package of squashed chips. She divided the chips, arranged them beside the chicken with the care of a dinner party hostess.

The boy looked at the plates with pride then and gave her one of his best quick grins. He asked if she wanted wood for the fire now. When he was gone over the edge of the mountain the man came to her and put his hand on her back but she kept dividing and arranging, rearranging and avoiding his eyes.

After supper they talked of more countries, sharing with the boy all the information they could summon, all they knew of places they'd been and hadn't been. On the return trip he led them, checking his facts as he brought them country by country, province by province, back to the fire on the top of the mountain. He said that he didn't think he'd like the prairies much and it made her catch her breath, made her concentrate for a tough minute on holding a placid face.

When the fire was out they stripped down to their underwear and settled into the sleeping-bags, leaving the tops unzipped, loose over them. The night air was gently cool. She lay facing the man for a few minutes and he stroked her hair, tried to rub the creases out of her forehead. He said she'd be happier. He didn't try to keep the caring out of his eyes and so, enraged, she turned to face the sky. Stars and light won out against the dark empty space, making it seem more distant than it was. She turned again then, toward the boy who was quiet beside her, his breathing regular and peaceful. She turned finally to the distance within her, turned to it for help against the need to fight, the need to stay. She cried without sound for most of the night. The man did not try to save her from it.

In the morning she woke to the smell of smoke from the breakfast fire and to an overwhelming sense of love being offered. When she came fully awake she recognized the love in the boy, sound asleep, curled warm and tight against the hollow of her body. And she knew she really would be leaving on Monday and she knew how careless they'd been to include the boy in their lives. And she became, there on top of the mountain, with the fire and the man and the boy, another aberration.

CRUSH

It's Thursday morning and it's hot, hot, hot. The girl is painting the kitchen cupboards. The paint stinks up the kitchen, stinks up the whole house. Her summer-blond ponytail and her young brown shoulders are hidden in the cupboards and a stranger coming into the kitchen, seeing only the rounded buttocks in the terrycloth shorts and the long well-formed legs, might think he was looking at part of a woman.

She's tired. She babysat last night. It isn't the best job she can get; there are other kids, easier kids. She takes the job because of him, because she loves to ride alone with him on the way home. He is Allen, the breadman; she thinks she loves him. She remembers him at the beach, throwing his kids around in the water, teaching them to swim. His back and thighs she will remember when she is 70 and has forgotten others. She does not try to imagine anything other than what she has seen. It is already more than enough.

Her mother stands over the ironing-board just inside the dining-room door. Thunk, hiss, thunk, hiss. The kitchen table separates them. It is piled high with dishes and tea-towels and bags of sugar and flour and pickling-salt. Jars of spices are pitched here and there, rest askew in the crevices of the pile. The cupboards are hot and empty. She has nearly finished painting the inside of them.

Neither the girl nor her mother has spoken for over an hour. It is too hot. She leans back out of the cupboards, unbuttons her blouse and takes it off, tossing it over to the table. It floats down over the dishes. She wants to take off her bra, but doesn't.

"You be careful Allen doesn't catch you in that state young lady. He'll be along with the bread soon." Her mother doesn't lift her head from the ironing. Her sleeve-less housedress is stained with sweat. It soaks down toward her thick waist.

Maybe I want him to, the girl thinks. She does not share this thought with her mother. Her mother doesn't know about backs and thighs.

"Have you picked out the bathing-suit you want?" Her mother glances up at her. The bathing-suit is to be the reward for the painting. "It's time you started thinking about modesty. It's beginning to matter."

"No." The girl drags the fresh blue paint over the old pale green. But she has picked out her suit. It's the one on the dummy in the window downtown, the one the boys stare at. She knows she won't be allowed to have it. Mrs. Stewart in the ladies shop wouldn't even let her try it on. Said it wasn't suitable for her. But it does suit her. She wants it.

She hears the scream of the ironing-board as her mother folds it up and again her mother's voice.

"I'm going downtown for meat. You put that blouse on before I leave."

"Why?" The girl looks at the limp skin on her mother's arm. "Nobody's here."

"Because Allen's coming with the bread soon, that's why. Now get it on. I'm as hot as you are and you don't see me throwing my clothes off."

Her mother stands checking the money in her purse, waiting till the last button is secure before she heads for the back door. "I'll bring you some cold pop." The screen door slams.

The girl steps down from the paint-splattered chair, goes to the sink, turns on the water and lets it run cold. She opens the freezer door, takes out a tray of ice cubes. She fills a glass with ice, slows the tap, watches the water lap around the ice cubes as it seeks the top of the glass. She drinks slowly. She isn't thirsty, but it's the only way to get something cold inside her. She pulls an ice cube out of the glass, holds it in her hand, feels it begin to melt against the heat of her palm. She raises her hand to her forehead, rubs the ice against her skin, back into her hair, over her neck, down into the sweaty shadow between her breasts. The ice cube is small now, just a round lump. Her hand is wet.

When he danced with her at the Fireman's dance, his hand was wet. Not the same wet though, not the same at all. His buddies hollered things about him liking the young stuff and they all laughed, even the wives. She laughed too, pretended she understood how funny it was, his touching her. But the skin on her back can still feel the pressure of his arm, how it moved her the way he wanted her to move. It should have been hard to move together. But it was easy, like a dream.

61

She wonders how close he is to their house. She dries her hand on the tea-towel hanging from the stove door. She undoes the top button of her blouse then the next and the next and the next. It falls from her hand in a heap on the floor. She unfastens her bra, slips it down over her brown arms, lets it drop on top of the blouse.

She climbs up on the chair, begins to paint again. She can't smell the paint anymore or feel the ache in her arm that the movement brings.

Turning, she sees him standing there in the kitchen with her, the basket of baking slung round his neck. She comes down from the chair, steps over the blouse and bra, stands in front of him, as still as the surface of a hot summer lake. There is no sound but the catch of his breathing, no movement but the startled rhythm of his eyes moving from her face to her warm bare skin and back again.

"Jesus," he says.

"I wanted to show you, that's all."

He goes out the door quickly, doesn't leave Thursday's two loaves of white and one wholewheat.

Her mother's voice at the door hits the girl like an iceberg. She stands frozen, knowing that she will be caught and that she will be punished. Punished in some new way. She bends down, picks up her bra.

He's in the truck and he's wishing he had further to go than the next block. Jesus. Bread to deliver. After that. What the hell was she trying to do.

He checks the rearview mirror. Maybe her mother thinks he was in on it; she could come roaring out after him any minute. He's a sitting duck in this damned truck. A drive. He'll go for a drive, just to clear his head. Christ.

He drives out past the gas station, past the local In and Out store, out of the town, onto a grid road. He goes a few miles, lets the hot breeze blow the sweat away. He pulls over.

His wife. What if it gets back to her? She'll find some way to blame him. He should go right now and tell her the truth. Shit. She wouldn't believe him. He doesn't believe it and he was there. He'll just lie low and hope, pray, that her mother is too embarrassed to tell anyone.

Her mother. What if she does think he was in on it? Maybe he should go back there right now, tell her straight out. She could watch his hands shake. No. If it's going to come up it'll come up soon and he'll just say it was a surprise and he won't be lying. Jesus.

The girl has never given him one small clue that she was thinking in those terms. She's a good kid. He enjoys talking to her and he always makes a point of being nice to her when he picks her up to sit and when he drives her home. She always hides herself behind a huge pile of books held up tight to her sweater. And she helped him teach the kids to swim 'cause his wife wouldn't and he didn't even look at her, can't even picture her in a bathing-suit.

So damned hot. He leans back in his seat, unbuttons his shirt, lights a cigarette. The sight of her comes back through the smoke that hangs around him. Not centrefold stuff, not even as nice as his wife before the kids but nice just the same, yeah, nice. It's been a long time since he's seen fresh, smooth, hard ones. He shifts around in his seat. Damn.

It's like she just discovered she had them. Or maybe she just got tired of being the only one who knew. Now he knows. And what's he supposed to do about it? Jesus. What she said made it sound like it was supposed to be some kind of gift. Man, this is too complicated for a Thursday morning.

The picture comes back again and this time he holds it and looks it over a little more carefully. He's sure they've never been touched. He thinks about dancing with her that once and how easy she was in his arms. Not sexy, just easy. Like she trusted him. He can't remember ever feeling that before. They sure didn't trust him when he was seventeen, had no business trusting him. And what he gets from his wife isn't trust, not exactly.

Kids are sometimes just crazy. That's it, she's crazy. But he remembers her eyes and whatever it was they were saying, it had nothing to do with being crazy.

Back the picture comes again and Jesus it is like a gift. He closes his eyes and the breasts stay in his eyes and he thinks he sees his own hands going to them and he feels a gentleness come into his hands and he sits up straight and he starts the truck and he tells himself you're crazy, man, that's who's crazy.

The mother stands watching the girl do up the last of the buttons on her blouse. She holds the package of meat in one hand, the bottle of pop in the other. The paper around the meat is dark and soft where blood has seeped out. She walks over to the fridge, puts the meat in the meat-keeper and the pop beside the quarts of milk on the top shelf. She closes the fridge door with the same care she would use on the bedroom door of a sleeping child. When she turns the girl has climbed up on the chair in front of the cupboard and is lifting the brush.

"Get down from that chair," she says.

The girl puts the brush across the top of the paint can and steps down.

"I could slap you," the mother says, calmly. This is not a conversation she has prepared herself for. This is not a conversation she ever expected to have. She cannot stop herself from looking at the girl's body, cannot stop the memory of her own body and the sudden remorse she feels knowing it will never come back to her. She longs for the sting of a slap, longs to feel it on her own hand and to imagine it on the girl's cheek. But she puts the anger someplace, out of the way. She pulls a chair from the table, away from the mess of cupboard things piled there and sits in the middle of the room, unprotected.

"Sit down," she says.

The girl sits where she is, on the floor, her brown legs tucked under her young bum as they were tucked through all those years of stories, fairy tales. But the mother can smell her fear.

"How much did you take off?"

The girl does not answer. She looks directly into her mother's eyes and she does not answer.

The mother begins the only way she knows how.

"I had a crush on your father. That's how it started with us, because I had a crush on him. He was only a little older than me but I think it's the same. I don't know why it should happen with you so young but I think it's the same. The difference is I didn't take my clothes off for him. And he wasn't married. It's wrong to feel that way about someone if he's married and it's wrong to take your clothes off. Do you understand?"

The girl picks at a scab on her ankle.

"The way you feel has got nothing to do with the way things are. You've embarrassed him. I could tell at the gate he was embarrassed. You won't be babysitting for them anymore. He'll tell his wife and they'll laugh about it. You've made a fool of yourself."

The girl lifts the scab away from her skin. The mother wants to pick her up in her arms and carry her up to bed.

"You will feel this way from now on. Off and on, from now on. You have to learn to live with it. I wish it hadn't happened so soon. Now you just have to live with it longer. Do you understand?"

The girl shakes her head no.

"Women have this feeling so they will marry, so they will

have children. It's like a system. And you've got to live within the system. There will be a young man for you, it won't be long. Maybe five years. That's all. You've got to learn to control this thing, this feeling, until that young man is there for you."

The mother gets up from her chair and goes to the fridge. She takes the pop out and opens it, divides it between two glasses. She hands one to the girl.

"If you don't control it you will waste it, bit by bit, and there will be nothing left. There will be no young man, not to marry. And they'll take it from you, all of them, any of them, because they can't stop themselves from taking it. It's not their responsibility. It's your responsibility not to offer it. You just have to wait, wait for the one young man and you be careful who he is, you think about it for a long time and then you marry him and then you offer it."

The girl gets up from the floor and puts her glass on the counter by the sink.

"Can I go now?" she asks.

The mother feels barren. She is not a mother anymore, not in the same way. It is as if the girl's undressing has wiped them both off the face of the earth.

The girl has run away from the house, out past the gas station and the beer store onto the grid road that divides the corn fields. She is sitting in a ditch, hidden, surrounded by long grass and thistles.

She likely has ruined it, likely will never babysit for them again. Not because he was embarrassed. He wasn't embarrassed, he was afraid. It's the first time she'd ever made anyone afraid. She will find a way to tell him that she didn't mean to make him afraid.

She wishes her mother had slapped her. She didn't like hearing about how her mother felt about her father, it was awful, and all that talk about controlling it and getting married someday, she knows all of that. That's what everybody does and it's likely what she'll do because there doesn't seem to be any way to do anything else. Except maybe once in a while. If she learns not to get caught. And not to scare anyone.

She feels really alone and she likes it. She thinks about his back and his thighs and she thinks about standing there in front of him. It's the best feeling she's ever had. She won't give it up. She'll just be more careful. She crosses her arms in front of her, puts one hand over each small breast and she knows she isn't wrong about this feeling. It is something she will trust. She leans back into the grass, throws her arms up over her head and stares, for as long as she can, at the hot July sun.

WINDOWS

I was thirteen the winter and spring I watched Miss Dickson. That was the year my brother went to university, the year I moved into the big bedroom. Her window, a movie screen rectangle, faced mine above the blue snow-covered lawns. My curtains were pale blue dotted swiss, tied back with velvet ribbon; she had drapes of pink and black, flamingoes in a dark swamp. She had a faded orange blind as well, a second assurance of privacy, but she never pulled the drapes and I could watch her easily through the blind, watch her silhouette, slightly enlarged, her angles, slightly distorted.

Miss Dickson was the new chemistry teacher and she

boarded with our neighbour, Mrs. Armitage. She had been hired at Christmas to replace the teacher whose steady pouring hands we had harrassed into clumps of quivering nerves. When Miss Dickson came into the lab that first day in January, it was obvious we wouldn't be doing her in. She walked back and forth across the front of the room, walked toward us, among us with a detachment and an odd half smile that promised nothing. She certainly wasn't friendly. The only friendly teachers in those days were the one who had no idea what they were doing. She was more like a competent machine, with just a hint of lustre.

Her suit was grey that first day, with narrow lapels and a walking-slit part way up the back of the skirt. And she had what I've come to know as a good haircut. Her hair was the same every minute of the day, a light auburn falling just so. It was only after she took off her suit jacket, only after I saw the glorious silk print that lined the jacket, all oranges and yellows and mauves, only then that I really looked at her face and saw that she was beautiful. And I saw that she didn't know she was beautiful, or if she had known, had forgotten.

Because she was so perfect, so easily perfect, I couldn't look at her without seeing myself standing beside her. Me with my twister ankle socks and my hot-pink pleated neck scarf, unavoidable evidence of the monstrous effort put into my appearance. Effort sustained by junk-filled closets, half-open drawers and a room littered enough to be dangerous, each new fad pushing the old ones deeper into forgotten corners. I stayed as far away from her as I could.

But I watched her with a passion. I wanted at my fingertips all the information, all the details that worked together to form such a woman. I was ready to learn. Each night, all that winter and spring, I gathered my books together and trudged upstairs, confusing my parents with this new found dedication. I arranged everything in a

69

precise muddle on my desk in case I should be caught by my mother, and I watched Miss Dickson as she sat across the way at her window, behind the blind.

For the first hour, that first January night of watching, she did school work. I was impatient for her to finish. I wanted her to do something real, maybe undress. Or pluck her eyebrows or file her nails, anything at all to preserve and perfect what she was for me. But she didn't. She got up and moved away from the window and then I saw the bathroom light come on. It was impossible to see anything; the bathroom window was high and small and frosted. When she came back to her room she had on a bulky robe and she sat down at her desk again. She worked for a while and then suddenly closed her daybook, grabbed the pen out of her mouth and threw it against the wall. Then she put her hands into her well-cut hair and she wrecked it. She walked to the closet, bent over into it and returned with a flask, just like the one my uncle carried inside his coat, and she drank from it, like a harlot, a delicate harlot. I felt the cold window pane on my forehead.

By the end of the second hour she was barely able to take off her robe and climb into bed. I lay awake in my own bed for a long time thinking I'd just seen what my mother quietly called a breakdown. Miss Dickson would not be in chemistry class the next day at all. She would still be in a drunken stupor or on the train, gone off somewhere, lost to me.

But she was there the next day, exactly the same as she'd been the day before. The only change was the colour of the suit; it was tan. The same cut, the same style, but tan. And again when she took her jacket off and put it over the chair at her desk, the lining made me catch my breath. There were circus scenes, circus animals, doing wonderful circus things.

That day after school I went to my mother's closet and found her suits, took the jackets off the hangers and examined the linings. They were all navy blue or brown. She came into the bedroom and asked what I needed with the inside of her jackets so I told her about Miss Dickson's linings and she laughed. She said Miss Dickson likely made her own suits and chose the material for the linings just to perk herself up a little. She asked what difference did it make. I didn't know.

There were three more suits, navy, brown and black but I studied the linings and kept track of them so I wouldn't be caught off guard anymore. The only one I didn't understand had big faces on it with all the noses and mouths and eyes out of place. I didn't spend much time looking at it, maybe just once or twice each time she took that jacket off.

I got more and more worried about the drinking. I watched closely every night, afraid she might be caught by Mrs. Armitage or pass out with a cigarette going and set her room on fire, be burned to death. I was afraid too that she might come to school some day still drunk and be fired in the hall in front of everyone by our bald little principal. But nothing happened. She was less delicate in the way she handled her flask, that's all. All through January and February and March she just kept wearing those suits with the crazy linings and becoming less and less delicate with her flask.

Then in April my mother was at a tea with Mrs. Armitage and learned that Miss Dickson's brother was going to visit her. He was supposed to be from Montreal and Mrs. Armitage was always, my mother quoted, delighted to get a chance to meet with someone from one of the larger cultural centres. My mother said he was likely a sanitation man, she said that's what they called them in the large cultural centres, and wouldn't Mrs. Armitage learn a lot. My mother was never very impressed with the unknown.

The brother was to come on a Sunday and I watched Miss Dickson all the nights leading up to that Sunday, hoping she might straighten herself around, hoping she would find his visit a way of breaking herself of what she was doing. Because she was beginning to spoil herself. Thick creases were forming across her forehead and dark purple shadows deepening under her eyes. But she didn't let up. She was constant against the orange of that blind, smoking, messing up her hair, pulling on her flask and dropping clumsily on the bed. I was even getting a little homework done, it was so much the same every night. And I was angry with her. I was nearly ready to ask for my own blind so I wouldn't have to see her anymore.

When the Sunday came she sat on Mrs. Armitage's verandah, waiting. I sat on ours, my feet propped up against the cement railing and my chemistry book prominently displayed against my legs. She had a big blue novel on her lap but I could tell she wasn't really reading. The warm air had already taken the winter smell away, and it made me want to be older. It made me wonder if there would ever be a spring when I could understand someone like Miss Dickson and maybe help her somehow. I didn't think about talking it all over, the way my mother sometimes did with her dizzy friends. I just thought about walking with her, with some kind of magical caring passing from me to her. I thought that windows were great for seeing through but pretty useless when it came to doing anything. Watching people through their windows wasn't rude, it was useless.

When the car finally pulled up there were two men in it, not just Miss Dickson's brother. As soon as she saw them she stood up and headed back across the verandah to the front door, but Mrs. Armitage was there, just coming out, so she was trapped. The man who looked like Miss Dickson took the verandah steps in two leaps, went right up to Miss

Dickson and hugged her. But she was stiff against the hug and turned her head away from the other man, the blond one.

Lord. He was as beautiful as she was. He even had a beard. He wasn't handsome like the goons in the movie magazines, he was just there, just perfectly there in his big blond way. And the way I loved her finally defined itself in him, in his face. He was what I wanted her to have.

Mrs. Armitage served tea and cupcakes. I got myself an Orange Crush from the fridge. Miss Dickson sat beside her brother, her hand tucked under his arm, staring at the maple trees that were coming into bud and occasionally looking over at me. She was fidgety and I had the feeling that she might stand up any minute and call me over.

When finally Mrs. Armitage left them, when she collected her china and her teapot and disappeared into the house, Miss Dickson's brother got up and followed her in. Miss Dickson and the blond man were alone, except for me. I thought maybe I should go into the house but I didn't. They could ignore me, surely. I wouldn't matter at all, it was so strong between them. They could talk low so I wouldn't hear. I had to see it. I had to see him touch her.

When he did touch her she let out a soft ugly scream and backed up against the railing of the verandah, her hands in front of her, pushing against him. And they didn't talk low. He talked about Jan, about Jan having an abortion, about it all being tidied up with Jan. Miss Dickson just kept yelling that was too damned bad, too damned bad. I ran for the door, leaving the sound of my breaking Orange Crush bottle behind me. My mother stopped me in the hall, said she was just coming out to talk to me. I didn't want to talk.

Screaming at the blond man must have helped Miss Dickson because she stopped drinking after that Sunday. Some nights when she was finished with her daybook she actually did file her nails and pluck her eyebrows. I filed my nails with her and I bought some witchhazel to kill the pain when I plucked my eyebrows but it still hurt so I quit. In May, my mother, in her oblivious way, fixed Miss Dickson up with my father's new partner. I couldn't help but see him call for her. My friends thought it was all so romantic and they pumped me for information but they didn't get any.

Miss Dickson didn't marry the young lawyer, though they looked really good together. She gradually appeared a little healthier, the suits continued in rotation and I learned a bit of chemistry.

In June, when it got really hot, she pulled her blind up and opened her window. I decided to move my desk; I didn't like being so exposed. I was standing, gathering everything up so I could pull the desk away from the window, and I looked over one last time. She stood in her own window, arranging herself so that she stood exactly as I stood, moved as I moved, putting her arms, her head, everything in the same position as mine. Then she waved and made a signal for me to wait, turning to get something from her dresser. She came back with a lipstick and she scrawled a message on her window. She wrote it backwards. It was smeary but big enough to read. It said I LOVE YOU TOO. Humiliation, immediate and deserved, started to move through me. But the words, red and clear, absorbed the humiliation in a way I still remember more exactly than any chemical experiment. I wanted to write something back and I got my lipstick but it was pale pink, too pale to make a message. I have no idea what I might have said.

I watched from our verandah when Miss Dickson's brother came to pick her up at the end of the year. She didn't come back. Mrs. Armitage said she was going back to teach in the city.

74

I'm teaching in a city now, French, not Chemistry, and Rick and I have come home to spend Christmas with my family. I'm not surprised to find my room has changed. The blue dotted swiss curtains are thin and washed out to near grey; the desk is small. Even my window is smaller than I remember it. I stand looking across the blue snow-covered lawn that separates my parents' house from Mrs. Armitage's. She still boards teachers; I hear the current one is a man, a very nice man from one of the larger cultural centres. I see the faded orange blind has been replaced with white venetians. The boarder thinks he's pulled them shut but thin yellow strips of light, parallel rows of them, escape. And there is a glow behind the blinds, a tantalizing glow. I sit down to wait, aware that I am framed in light against the winter night and its darkness.

REFLECTIONS

He calls her Mother and she calls him Dad. They have separate bedrooms. They begin each day by saying good morning when they meet in the kitchen for breakfast, fully dressed. In their nightclothes, they are an embarrassment to each other. If they happen to meet on the way to the bathroom before breakfast, there is no acknowledgement. For 47 years they have lived together. He sometimes tries to remember a time when it was not like this, but that time is gone.

They have come here to the cemetery at her insistence, to locate their plots. There's not much to face together anymore but there is this one thing. Or two things if you count each death separately. One of them, he knows, will go first, will have just the one death. But the other will have to go through two. The only thing worst would be a son or daughter going, dying, before them. He winces at the thought. He knows he doesn't have the strength, could never find the strength, to bury any of the children. He's seen a couple of friends do it, right here in this cemetery and it was worse than torture to watch. He and Mother buried one, a long time ago, but it was just an infant and they were young and had the other kids and the promise of more. No. One death, possibly two, that's all he could manage now.

He parks the Olds in the overgrown edge of the grass by the barbed-wire fence. She gets out as if she's anxious to see what's ahead, checking her small flowered notebook for the instructions she got from the town clerk this morning. He sits in the car a minute, his big brown arm hanging out the window. He surveys the rows of massive old maples surrounding the place. There is room for shafts of sunlight to move through the maples, and his eyes follow them to the faces of the tombstones where they explode. "What a bloody waste of sunlight," he mutters.

She's already 30 yards away. She motions with her arm for him to follow, doesn't turn, just keeps on walking, one hand holding the notebook, the other waving him on. He watches the cardigan sweater responding to the swinging of her hips. He's never told her about the swinging of her hips.

He dreams her young with a waist so small he can wrap his hands around it. She is quiet and astoundingly elegant in a cloche hat and a mauve dress that reminds him of a meadow. Only her shoes are practical, sensible. She is a quiet mauve cloud, and he has to assume when she doesn't say no that she means yes.

He opens the heavy car door, thinks about a heart

attack. That's what's most likely for him now. Two out of four brothers have gone that route already. A stroke would be all right as long as he doesn't live through it, doesn't find himself alive without a mind, or movement or speech. He shuns all other possibilities. He thinks of young people when he thinks of cancer. Leukaemia, lung cancer, those are for the young.

By the time he catches up to her, she has stopped in front of a pinkish stone. Before she can speak, he reads it, sees that it's Geordie Arnott for God's sake, Geordie Arnott who damned near got to her before he did, when they were young. Him with his manners and his soft womany voice. He charges on past her toward the area of the cemetery where their plots are supposed to be, where the leaves blow freely across the open expanse of grass.

He can't imagine what will take her. She's always been so small, been so vulnerable, like a young calf. But nothing ever hurt her much. She had four of the kids right on the kitchen table, so many years ago now that it seems to him she just stopped ironing or scrubbing, jumped up on the table when the doctor came, went to bed for a day or two, then carried right on ironing or scrubbing. He has to admit he's no authority on those times. She would go into herself, and then the baby would take her until it could toddle around by itself, sit at the table with them. And by then there would be another.

He dreams a child in woollen soakers with lovely fat thighs. He calls the child Pudge, and his eyes water as he heaves him high in the air over his head, thinking how solid, how strong, how goddamned miraculous this thing is.

He continues to walk, turns and walks back toward their plots. She is pausing here and there, reading inscriptions, pulling her cardigan tight around her small frame. She is pulling weeds away from the base of a stone he should recognize, but doesn't. It's a friend, he just can't remember which one.

Five years. If he was a betting man, he would put money on them both being dead within five years. The same span of time their sons are counting on to get their houses paid off, their pensions fattened up. No ignoring it. All you have to do is look around downtown, count the faces that were there last year, aren't there now. Lord knows he's had his suit out often enough in the last few years, and it hasn't been for christenings. The doctor says he has to stop thinking this way, has to stop dwelling on it. Says he should eat a little less too, and give up hauling the firewood in from the bush, as if it's all the same kind of thing.

Stop dwelling on it. Sure thing. He wished he could take the doctor to that picture they saw last month when their daughter took them to the gallery in the city. It was a horse on some railroad tracks, and behind him, coming at him, was a train, a dark ugly iron-horse. The neck muscles were the biggest he'd ever seen on a horse, strained one against the other, not knowing whether to put their force into moving forward or looking back. And the hooves of that animal were suspended in the air, all four of them, and you just knew he'd never get his footing, never be able to dig in and get the hell out of the way of that thing bearing down on him. And he felt for that horse, knew how it was for that horse, could barely make himself look at the eyes painted on the face of the beast. He knew how wild they'd be. If he could get the doctor there, in front of that painting, he'd tell him to tell the horse to stop dwelling on that train, the noise of it, the force of it, coming down on him from behind. He'd tell the doctor that if the horse agreed, he'd agree.

He is in the new area now, leaning against one of the maples that shades it. He looks back to the rows and rows of tombstones, and if she were not among them, wandering around, he would easily see the cemetery grown out in all directions, reproduce itself a hundred times and become a memory of those other cemeteries.

He dreams a war and a young man. The young man rides in the back of a truck. Bumping around beside him are guns and two dead friends. He is screaming with pain but the bombs continue anyway and the shrapnel rains around him. The truck stops, and someone comes to him and rams a needle in his ass and ahh...this is morphine and it feels so good, feels so much better than the slow leaking away of his blood. Because he doesn't want it to leave, not all of it.

She's a lot more practical about death. She went over to the town clerk this morning, bought these plots for them, like twin beds. And last week she went to the tombstone dealer and chose their stone, had it engraved with their names and the dates of their births. She took him over when it was finished, made him look at it, but all he could see was the part that was left off, the spaces for the dates still to be chiselled into the granite. She wanted him to pay for it then and there, but he told them to bill him. He'd be damned if he'd stand over his own tombstone and write out a cheque for it. It took him a long time to forgive her that little practicality, and now here they are, pretending that choosing the plot of land that will be dug up for them and thrown back over them is like choosing the damned house when they moved into town from the farm. Sometimes he suspects the blood runs cold through her small body, cold and thin, never slowing, never thickening with warmth for a minute. He knows this isn't fair, caught on a long time ago that it's no use hating her for what she seems to be doing or saying, no use judging her in any ordinary way. You just have to trust her, take the air she gives you and warm it yourself before you breathe it in.

Two of the kids have her way about them: the daughter who will never look at you or touch you, the son who turns everything to ice with his analyses. It broke his heart when he first saw it. But he loves them none the less, treats them equally with the others. And he's locked away on velvet cushions in his mind all the happy times with them, because they were so few.

She's coming over to him now, her head down, her steps on the path determined. He dreams a bride on his arm with the face of his wife, but her waist is thick, thick with a grandchild for him. "The Wedding March" booms around them and he can feel her arm shaking in his as they start down the aisle, but she will not look at him, will not acknowledge that they are together in any way.

He moves away from the maple and stands behind her, reading the notebook over her shoulder, and he feels the blood leave his head. 1038 and 1093, what the hell kind of joke is this? But she is laughing, saying she just copied it down wrong, telling him to watch for the numbers on the stakes that are pounded into the ground at regular intervals. "Shit!" he shouts, taking an awkward old man's run at the line of stakes, kicking at them as he goes. Shit, snap, shit, snap, until only one or two are left whole, the rest broken. The jagged splints expose fresh light-coloured wood. He feels winded and content. She ignores him. She bends over one of the stakes, pieces it back together so she can read the number on it. "Just settle yourself," she says.

Three of the kids have his way about them. They've always brought a madness, a spur-of-the-moment kind of nonsense to everything that goes on, and he grins at the thought of them. They live full throttle. They have ups and downs more interesting than the ones he watches on the soaps every day. But the other two, she and the other two, live in some place that never changes, some place you couldn't find if you spent your whole life looking.

He dreams a search through cobwebs, through dust and dry stale air. He doesn't know what he's looking for and he wishes he had some help.

He tried to tell her about this one night when they were in the same warm bed together, but she cried, said he frightened her with his demands. Said she didn't live any place that ordinary people didn't live, and couldn't he just see it as her way of getting through things. She said you could roar and jump around and laugh out loud or you could do it all privately, to yourself. He understood then for a little while, was willing to call what he felt "understanding." And he tried to pull her to him, but she pulled away and cried more, had to leave the bed to get herself settled down.

"Here we are," she says, and he storms back across the cemetery, careless of his path, walking obstinately over graves, cheerfully patting tombstones as he swings himself around them, thinking not yet we aren't, not yet.

In a few minutes she is beside him in the car, doing up her seatbelt, tucking her notebook into her purse. He does not say he is sorry, he stopped saying he was sorry years ago. She would only respond, you should be, the anger in the words, never in the soft perfect face.

He dreams her at the bedroom mirror, an old woman in her nightgown, with her back to him. His eye catches the still small outline of her waist, and he can see the freckled shoulders clearly, but her face will not form itself. He sees the children's faces fading in and out of focus where hers should be, and once he sees his own face there, but never hers. He longs to gently mould the features, make her come alive for him, but he can't approach her. He is tangled in the messy, rumpled bed.

And they will die soon, he knows, and he can see three of the kids standing motionless over a grave, raging against it, hating it, as they should. The other two will be dull-faced, doing whatever they are doing privately, to themselves.

If it is to be her standing with the children over his grave, she will be quiet and controlled, maybe admiring the damned tombstone. And he will be somewhere floating about them, somehow absolved by the grief of the grieving, somehow abandoned by the silence of the others.

But if it is to be him standing with them over her grave, he will sense her in the air around him, holding him, he will feel her final silence and he will go mad with missing her, mad with it.

He does not know why his face moves into a grin.

He calls her Mother and she calls him Dad. They have separate bedrooms. They begin each day by saying good morning when they meet in the kitchen for breakfast, fully dressed. In their nightclothes they are an embarrassment to each other. If they happen to pass on the way to the bathroom before breakfast, there is no acknowledgment. For 47 years they have lived together. She sometimes tries to remember a time when it was not like this, but that time is gone.

She has finally got him down to the cemetery to locate their plots. It wasn't something she particularly wanted to do alone. But truth be told they will both die soon. First one, then the other. It can't be avoided. She supposes, has always supposed, that there is something after death, something for the energy, the spirit, to become. She has always supposed too that the child they buried long ago existed still somehow. It makes no difference that she can't imagine how or where. It is nice to dream that he has been all this time in someone's arms, that he will be shown to her, returned to her, but she knows that to be a foolish dream. A perfect leaf drifts down from one of the maples edging the cemetery, lands on her shoulder, sticks to the wool of her cardigan. She picks it off, takes the hard stem in her fingers, twists it, watching the colour spin. He's still in the car. She wishes he wouldn't brood so. She's so tired of all the dramatic phrases: six feet under, three score and ten, final resting-place, and on and on. That's the talk at home, and now they're here, right in the middle of everything, he's got nothing to say.

She doesn't look back, just waves him on, knowing he'll be watching her to see if she'll do it. Then she hears the car door open, pictures his big frame emerging from the car. It's always reminded her of one of those circus clowns getting out of an undersized, almost toy, car. He doesn't shut the door.

She dreams him young with shoulders so wide they make her believe in him. He is all movement and strength, all power and lust and confidence. He makes her feel like a ripe garden peach pulling a branch to earth with the weight of its juice. And she is not afraid of his teeth, not yet.

She feels the pull in her groin as she walks, slips her hand under her cardigan to rub it. She's got to see about it. It's been going on too long. She blocks from her mind the picture of the organs she knows to be inside her there, doesn't want to know the particulars. If this small constant pain is to be the beginning of her dying, that's fine, she'll handle it the best she can. She'll see about it.

To her left, in the old part of the cemetery, half-way down the slope to the cornfield beyond, rest her father and her son. She won't go down today. One thing at a time. They're here on business. She does notice a beautiful marble stone three or four feet in from the path, and she goes over to it. It's pinkish in the sunlight, and she can see her image reflected in it, clear as day. He's almost beside her, and she thinks it would be nice to be reflected together on a warm autumn day like this, but he's gone, charging off like some mad old bull. Then she reads the inscription and sees it's Geordie Arnott. Surely he wouldn't think she was standing here mooning over Geordie Arnott. He had been a lovely suitor, but he didn't turn out all that well, and Dad couldn't think she would trade her life for life with Geordie, not hardly. But he's off, mad about something that's nothing more than nonsense.

He will have a heart attack, she is sure. He's got too heavy since he gave up the farm, won't quit eating like an adolescent. She could spank him. If she doesn't cook potatoes, he invites her for a walk after supper, steers them directly to the new drive-in restaurant and wolfs down a double order of those greasy french fries. And since she stopped baking pies and cakes, he's fallen head over heels in love with Sara Lee. Her eyes clamp shut at the image of him clutching his chest, bellowing out his pain. She will call the ambulance and hold his hand as tight as she can, but it won't be enough, won't stop anything.

She notices another stone, Laura Blain's. Born 1908. died 1943. Half a life. They went through the baby years together. She shakes her head to get the thoughts out of it. There are weeds around the base of the stone, and she pulls them up, every one of them, by the roots.

She remembers the pain of having the children. Knows it was nothing, nothing like what the pain of death might be. But it hurt, just the same. And she remembers the doctor's eyes, challenging her to bear the pain, and she did bear it, would not have screamed out if it had killed her, partly to show what she was made of, but more because she was worried about the child being rammed up against her pelvis. She could see the unborn baby, small and quivering, terrified at the force being used against it, unaware of the light ahead of it.

She dreams a child in woollen soakers with skin that seems to melt under her touch, it's that soft. She laughs at her own pleasure in handling him. And he is brave like his father, not afraid of stairs or cars or dogs or fire. She feels a tug of pride in his confidence, but still she had to teach him that he is not invincible, share some of her own fear with him so he will know when to back away from things.

Straightening up now, she sees him over by the fence, leaning against the trunk of a maple tree. His arms are folded across his chest, and he's kicking at the leaves absently. She wonders how many autumns will come for them, how many more seasons. Four times five, four times four, four times three? She knows she must never count them out for him. He's reacting so badly to things, made a terrible scene at the gallery last month, in front of that painting. She was mortified. He says he's going to tell the doctor about that horse, to help him understand how a man feels. He'll be lucky if he doesn't get himself a prescription for Valium. She knew immediately what the painting might mean for him, but it was too late. She had to stop herself from exploring the horrors in the thing. Instead she looked at the frame, thought it would be better a little wider, mentioned this to their daughter. The girl threw her head back in exasperation, huffed away in a display almost equal in intensity to her father's agony.

She starts walking through the rows of stones toward him. She dreams him gone to war. There are two children at her feet and she is knitting socks. The children ask if the socks are for Daddy, and she says yes they are, knowing full well that thousands of socks are being knitted at this moment, and that thousands of feet are cold and bleeding somewhere, and that it doesn't much matter which socks go on which feet. The faster she knits, the better the chance his feet will be warmed.

She thinks only of his feet.

She notices a stone much like the one she chose last week for them. The bill for it came this morning. He tossed it across the table at her, said it gave him the chills. She isn't sorry, though, isn't sorry they are here today finding their plots. It wouldn't be right to leave it for the children to do. She's seen the children of friends over their parents' graves, and she marvelled at the quiet bond between them. A bond made of ordinary things like memories and shared houses and just the same last name. She doesn't want practicalities to spoil that bond for their own children.

They find themselves at funerals on a regular basis now. She has to keep a small supply of tarts and loaves in the freezer. At the funeral parlours he hugs whoever comes to him for hugging, mostly kids he's watched grow from infancy to middle age. And he watches the ones who don't come to him, watches them for signs, reflections of his own feelings.

Three of their own kids are great huggers, and they have his other ways about them too. They rage and roar around, have done so from the time they could first hold their balance as toddlers. It's never solved anything, but you couldn't tell them that. They court chaos. Still, they're good to have around, in moderate doses. When they're happy they bring everyone into it, like dancers pulling more partners to the floor.

She dreams a child who has failed a year at some far-off university. He is incensed at the injustice he has been served. She suspects he has been lazy and that he will be able to admit this to himself eventually, but first there must be a three-act play exploring his feelings about the failure. He charges from one side of the stage to the other, playing to her, watching for her reaction. But she gives none. She can neither laugh nor cry and she will not applaud. It's his play and his alone. She knows nothing about the theatre.

Where's the page now, where's the page with their plot numbers? She leafs through the notebook, turns past the birthday section and the anniversary section. The notes she took this morning are at the back, under P, for plot.

The other two kids are more like her. She is comfortable with them. They seem content with their lot and have been a help to the others in an ordinary, stable way. She does regret there is so little between them and their father, wishes they could meet his warmth with something of their own.

She dreams a party. Everyone but her and two of the children seem to be drunk with something, and they are dancing around, clapping their hands high above their heads and stomping, circling the three of them tighter and tighter. She senses there is some special thing they could do to escape, and she asks the others if they know what it is, but they don't. She thinks maybe they are expected to join the dancing and she tries, but her rhythm is off. She feels frightened and very foolish.

She is with him now, near the plots. He stands behind her, reading the notebook over her shoulder. She points to the numbers, 1038 and 1093 and she feels his terror on her neck. She laughs and says she copied it down wrong, of course it's 1039, 1038 and 1039. She asks him to watch for the numbers marked on the stakes pounded into the ground at regular intervals. And he's off, like an old maniac he's swearing, running down the row of stakes, kicking at them, cursing, breaking them off, crack, crack, crack, huffing and puffing and half tripping. Sometimes she suspects he doesn't have blood running through his veins at all, but lava, lava spilling out from some exploding core. Maybe that's where the heat comes from. He gives off a heat that exhausts, exhausts and frightens, because it really can damage more than stakes. "Just settle yourself," she says.

She knows she should move back into their bedroom, even if he hasn't asked her to. The day she moved her clothes over to the other bedroom, he asked what the hell was going on, but when she tried to explain he got her sewing-shears and cut one of her good Christmas nighties to pieces. Then he left, left the back door banging in the wind against the wall of the house. She was firm nevertheless. She couldn't talk anymore about death, about loneliness and things ending. It wasn't as if she were leaving him.

One night when they were still in the same warm bed together, she had had to turn her back to him, leave the bed finally, and she doesn't want that to happen again. Now she goes to him when she is sure there is no black mood, and they have good chats while she rubs his back.

She has, by piecing the stakes back together, one at a time, found their plots. "Here we are," she says. And he's off again, raging back to the car, stumbling in and out among gravestones, walking *over* some of the graves. He doesn't know how he hurts her, he can't know.

She dreams him in their bed, and she is at the bedroom mirror. Turn around, he says, turn around. But she is looking at her own face, examining the lines and shadows and hollows. Bring your face to me, he calls, I will tell you what it means. She cannot turn.

When she gets back to the car, she sees he is sitting behind the steering-wheel, his hands white with the force of his grip. She gets in, does up her seatbelt, and tucks her notebook into her purse. She is weak with anger.

And now they have to die. She can see two of the kids standing motionless over the grave. Their thoughts leak out through their eyes, and she is proud of their thoughts. The other three are sobbing, their breathing irregular, their thoughts without order.

If it is to be him standing with them over her grave, he will want their support. Those shoulders will heave, and he won't stand straight. And she will be somewhere floating above them, wishing she could hold the grieving ones, knowing the others can make their own comfort.

But if it is to be her standing with them over his grave, she will sense him the air around her, holding her, will hear his joy or his rage and she will miss him, she will miss him.

She glances over to him, the one she will miss, and she sees on his outrageous face the beginning of a grin. She cannot, though she tries with all the might she can muster, contain herself. She is roaring with it, her head thrown back, her hand on her stomach and her teary eyes on him. She is laughing.

SHARON SPARLING

THE CHINESE COAT

Chloe unzipped the clothing-bag, removed the Chinese coat, and lay it across the foot of the bed. It was pure silk, inside and out. The colour was graduated: pale cream at the shoulders, descending to a darker shade at the hem—the luminescent green on the underside of a wave in the sunshine. Two deep slits worked their way up the flared body of the coat, and the sleeves widened to a broad sweep at the wrist. The embroidery was in a faded yellow thread; a small wave pattern at the border; a blanket of wild chrysanthemums overall. It fastened down the front with spherical brass buttons in the shape of buds.

Laurence would be home soon. The sitter would arrive at 7.30, perhaps 7.25 —she was very conscientious. Andy was busy in his room playing with Lego. If one could succeed in building Lego into an amorphous mass, Andy had succeeded. All the other toys were placed neatly on the shelves that lined one wall. The exception was Bert, who occupied a place of honour on the upper bunk. Andy didn't play with dolls anymore, only the Lego. She hadn't had much experience with children before Andy. He was lost in the architectural wonder of the little bricks. She stared at him and pondered her continuing suspicion that he was unlike other five-year-olds. Maybe she should stop taking the pill. Would Laurence talk her into another abortion?

They had been married in the period when strict adherence to social convention was not only regarded as passé, but distinctly frowned upon. They bowed to the pressure of the times by not making a fuss about it. She wore a gown of a dusky Oxford blue, and wanted only to exchange vows. His mother's engagement-ring was taken from the safe-deposit box for a token wearing, and returned when the bank opened the next morning. Laurence found her a soupy antique emerald ring and convinced her that if she wore it on the middle finger, all the factions would be satisfied. She found herself agreeing, and rushed around until she found him a ring. It was a mourning ring with black enamel on gold, inscribed:

Marie Billings
Obit 1815
87 years

Laurence was tickled pink and insured it for $500. She had paid $90. He wore it on his baby finger. The enamel chipped off a few years later while he was playing squash, and it sat unrepaired in his cuff-link box with the dress studs and odd buttons she never got around to sewing back on his shirts. She rarely bothered wearing her ring. It distracted her when she played the piano.

She could scarcely remember when she hadn't played. Her father had been on the board of a small private school, now defunct, and the kindergarten section had been full, so they stuck her in grade one where there was a space. She was the youngest, the smallest and the dumbest. It had been a year of pain and isolation. Every afternoon she had come home, shut the door to her room, and cried for an hour or two, playing records on a small player. Her parents heard only the music so they assumed she had an interest and started her on the piano. Within months she was playing the early pieces of Mozart, to the delight of her parents. One day at school she started playing before the bell, and to her astonishment the entire class clustered around her in rapt attention.

She began to see that through accomplishment she might gain acceptance, but by the year's end she still hadn't learned to read. The only letters she could recognize were C, D, E, F, G, A and B, so she was held back. Looking through her files she had come across her report cards. She had been absent 44 days that year. Andy was reading at three and hadn't been sick a day in his life.

The Chinese robe had been an engagement present. It was antique too. She wasn't sure if it was a man's or a woman's; the Chinese were all so small. Probably smaller a century ago. did Chinese men wear robes with flowers embroidered all over? Probably a large woman, by Chinese standards. A tall woman with little bound, deformed feet encased in tiny red silk shoes. She would have sat around the house all day, in an ornamental sort of way, because it would have been too painful to walk. Her fingernails would have been long, her hands smooth and white.

Chloe bit her nails because she couldn't stand the sound of nails clicking on the keys as she played, and her fingers were long, although not particularly elegant. She had read that the most important feature of the bound foot was its effect on the sex life. It was said that a woman could be brought to orgasm merely by having them caressed, that men were driven wild by the odour they exuded, and liked to suck them; preferably without bindings, but more usually with. She found this fascinating. Pain was inextricably tied to pleasure. Submissive little bound feet touched the hem of this very robe.

"Mommy, Mommy, look what I made." The grey eyes that implored her were Laurence's. If she hadn't been in on the delivery, she might have doubted she'd had anything to do with this child. He wasn't at all like her. She was dark and brown-eyed, and he was fair like Laurence. It was unfair really. He came from a family of what seemed like a hundred people, and she was adopted. The very least God could've done was given her a kid who looked like her.

"I'm going to need some more Lego, Mommy. I'm running out."

"But sweetheart, you can take them apart and start over." There was already more than a hundred dollars invested in this digital, amoebic mess. She couldn't see the point to it all. It didn't look like anything.

"No, I can't. This is a new world. I need more."

He didn't whine, or make it sound like a demand. It was a matter-of-fact statement. She sighed. Like Laurence, he could make any request, no matter how outrageous, seem reasonable. If, five years ago, she had gone ahead with the pregnancy in defiance of Laurence's wishes, Andy would have a sibling upstairs right now, plucking apart Andy's blessed Lego and scattering it to oblivion. She couldn't argue with people like them, so convinced of the rightness of their positions. Opposition was pointless. She said nothing.

Laurence liked sex. He liked enthusiastic, gymnastic sex with a slim, agile partner. Her pregnancy had cramped his style. Two pregnancies in two years was one more than he would tolerate. It had taken her a few years to divine the real reason he had talked her into ending it.

"Where are you and Daddy going tonight?"
    "The museum."
    "Can I go too?"
    "No. It's past your bedtime."
    "It's Friday night..."
    "Oh good. Then I'll take you to see the exhibition tomorrow, after the library." He frowned at the floor for a moment. She had a fleeting desire to hug him, and felt guilty when it passed.
    "And we'll go to McDonald's for lunch, okay?"
    He stared at her with no expression in particular and wandered back to the new world in his bedroom.

The museum show was quite a coup for the director. On display was the largest collection of archaeological artifacts ever to leave the People's Republic, and it included a good representation of recent finds from the city of Xing. She had wanted to wear her black dress. It made her feel inconspicuous, but if anyone did notice her, it was a flattering cut. Laurence had convinced her that the Chinese coat would be more appropriate. She didn't doubt it. Half the people there would be wearing a Chinese something or other. It would be a bloody uniform.

She lay down on the thick red living-room carpet and dug her fingers into the pile. She had put nail-polish on for the first time in months. It was the same shade as the rug. She had bought it because it was a comfortingly familiar colour. It drew attention to the stubbiness of her nails. The cleaning-lady had been and vacuum tracks still criss-crossed the carpet. Chloe loved the place when it was all clean, shiny and dusted. She didn't want to go to the museum. She wanted to stay home and curl up in the fat armchair beside the fire with a sleazy book and some Bristol Cream. Just like an ad. She would encourage Laurence to go alone, and cancel the sitter. He would have a late dinner with friends and she would have five hours of peace. She would be asleep by the time he returned and he wouldn't dare wake her. The rug felt pleasantly rough against her cheek.

"Why are you lying on the rug, Mommy?"

Why are you lying on the rug, Mommy? Why, for God's sake, didn't he simply pounce on her like any other kid? She turned her head and there he was in his bright red Oshkosh overalls, staring at her like a suspicious policeman.

"Because it seemed like the best place to be at this particular moment."

"Oh, I see." Did he? Did he see? Or was he just trying to make things less awkward for himself?

"Do you want to come see my new world?"

"I saw it an hour ago, darling."

"But I've finished the cave of unrepentant spirits."

Where on earth did he pick up that concept? She and Laurence were atheists and his school was non-denominational. Wasn't it Descartes who, all by himself at the age of five, huddled in bed at night, had discovered, by his own efforts, most of the geometrical propositions? Was Andy a theological prodigy? What a repulsive idea.

"Okay, honey. I'll come in a minute."

He turned and walked up the stairs. He never ran up or down. Did other mothers dream of having a child like hers?

She yanked a loose thread from her dressing-gown and sat down at the piano. Laurence was in the shower. She had not yet told him that she wanted to stay home. Her fingers automatically fell on the opening chords of a Chopin nocturne. She played absent-mindedly, her eyes wandering about the room. She had annexed half the third floor for a studio, knocked out a wall, installed skylights, and moved her old rosewood Chickering grand up from the living-room. She loved the austerity of the space; it opposed the clutter of Laurence's ancestral things on the lower floors. The carpet was a pale beige, the walls a shade darker. She shunned window shades, and the glass disappeared in the indigo twilight. The only furnishings in the room were the piano and bench, and several delicate brass shelf units, stacked with sheet music. If anyone wanted to listen to her play, they had to sit on the floor. On one wall, facing the piano, was an oil painting; a seascape, undistinguished and unsigned. She had found it in a junk shop in France on their honeymoon, and had been attracted by the way the anonymous artist had captured the elusive quality of light before a storm. It had cost her twenty francs. Laurence balked when she spent $200 on custom framing. She paid for it herself. The lighting in the room was supplied by the window, the skylights and an oil lamp. The piano lived under one skylight and a weeping Java fig under the other. Curled yellow leaves littered the rug around the fig's base.

She had thought she was doing Laurence a favor by bringing music into his home. He didn't even have a stereo when she met him. She had been studying at McGill, and although he attended her recitals he never discussed music with her. She assigned it to natural reticence, and after they married she played for him in the evenings while he read. She was determined to impress him, and although she had always had an indifferent sort of discipline, she took to practising long hours during the day. The woman in the next house, a retired concert pianist, heard her and offered to give her lessons. Laurence seemed pleased and encouraged her to accept. That had been after the abortion.

Andy was weaned on Scriabin and Debussy. Still, Laurence declined to talk music with her. She realized with a shock one day that she had never heard him sing. Not even hum, or whistle. When she asked him about it, he said that he couldn't. She didn't believe him. Anyone could sing. She asked him to try the opening bars of "O Canada," and sure enough he couldn't stay on key. He was tone-deaf. Hard on this revelation, she moved the piano to the attic.

Her hands moved effortlessly over the keys, through the nocturne, into Ravel's "Pavanne for a Dead Princess," then "La plus que lente" by Debussy. She was half-way through when she heard the stairs creak, and the whine of the door being pushed open. She hated it when Laurence violated her space. Like an atheist in church, he didn't belong here. She tried to mask her indignation but was afraid her fingers would betray her. She hoped her voice would sound natural.

"What brings you to the inner sanctum?"

"You."

"So, what should I wear tonight?"

"I though we'd decided on the Chinese coat."

"With pants or a dress? Or naked underneath?"

He had come dripping up the stairs in his bathrobe, his wet feet leaving dark impressions on her pale carpet. She could feel him staring at her as she played. A chill ran down her spine. She hated being stared at. And he was smiling. That meant he wanted something.

"That would be nice." He put his hands on her shoulders and kissed the back of her neck.

"Which?"

"Naked. We could sneak into a dark corner with the ecclesiastical art and I could plank you against the wall."

"Or a convenient statue. I think the black satin pants. Which shoes though?"

"How 'bout the spiky black heels we got you last year?"

"Well, for one thing, the last time we wore them, we had to carry us home from Place des Arts."

"I remember."

"We were crippled for a week."

"You're very alluring when you limp."

"You're sick."

"And you love every minute of it, don't you?"

"Do I?"

"You'll wear the black heels and cling to my arm like a helpless lily. You can hobble through the halls of culture, wobble down the stairs. If I'm lucky you'll go flying and twist your ankle. That could mean two weeks in bed."

"Wouldn't that be just too convenient?"

"Hmm."

"If you like the damned things so much, you wear them."

"Killjoy."

"Sadist." She realized that while they were talking, she had progressed halfway through the "Revolutionary Etude."

"Laurence, would you mind awfully if I stayed home tonight? I don't know that I'm up to the culture-monger-ing hordes."

"And deny me the opportunity to show you off? Not a chance." He slid his hand through the open front of her dressing-gown and kneaded her breast. She felt his body press into her back.

"Not now, sweetie."

"Yes, now."

"Andrew is still up."

"He's busy with the new Lego I brought home."

"You spoil him. He has a ton of Lego already."

"Don't change the subject." He slipped his arm under her knees and lifted her off the piano bench.

"You'll smear my make-up."

"I won't go near your face." He immediately contradicted himself by kissing her dead on the mouth. There was no point in arguing.

She was still flushed from lovemaking, and didn't know whether to put on more rouge or not. She had restyled her long dark hair into a smooth cap ending in a coiled bun at the nape of her neck. She stood before the vanity mirror and dabbed perfume on her temples and behind her ears where the golden studs were just visible. She wore no other jewellery. The coat was ornament enough. She stared at her reflection for a long time without blinking, and after a while it wasn't Chloe, but another woman staring back with sad dark eyes.

She had checked her cape and boots and was pulling the cream shoes over thin nylon socks. They were Laurence's socks and the heels reached her ankles. Fortunately the pants fell over them and no-one would notice. A woman in the check line surveyed her robe and nodded, almost imperceptibly. Chloe felt gratified. It was easy to win appreciative glances from men—a little cleavage, a little thigh...but women—that was praise worth having. Laurence came toward her, smiling, and they climbed the stairs together. A cluster of people stood around the bar with drinks in hand, and she waited on the fringe while Laurence battled through. She was acutely conscious of being stared at and tried to appear nonchalant. A man in a dinner jacket started toward her, but she made a great show of examining a carving in a glass case, and he turned away. The piece was a lotus jar in white jade (what was it called? camphor jade?), not unlike the merchandise in Gump's catalogue, and she had a vague idea what her birthday present might be that year. Laurence approached her with two glasses of red wine. He was grinning.

"Do you believe that tux over there?" She recognized a local celebrity wearing a remarkably gaudy brocade suit with an overall design of dragons.

"He certainly looks silly."

"I expect someone paid him to wear it."

"I should hope so. He has to get some compensation for his humiliation." She noticed that he was also wearing gold ballet slippers. When he kissed some man in green leather, full on the mouth, she turned and headed for the exhibition rooms.

Chloe saw a familiar smile across the room, and a hand waved to her above the crowd. Laurence had posed her next to a display case containing T'ang horses. The yellow-and-green glaze dripping down their flanks complemented the colours in her robe.

"Did you see Mrs. Leander's face? She collects antique Chinese robes and she was lusting for ours."

She didn't hear. The thin, curly-haired man was angling toward her, his lady in tow. Laurence clutched her hand.

"Who's that?"

"Adam Carothers. He taught me composition in college. We used to go together."

"You never told me that."

"It never came up."

Adam embraced her and kissed her lightly on the cheek.

"You look as beautiful as ever. Nice coat."

He looked surprised. Did he expect she had descended into frumpery in the intervening years?

"Thank you. You're looking pretty good yourself. Lose weight?"

"Twenty pounds. This is Monique Boisvert. *Monique, mon amie Chloe, et son mari...*"

"*Laurence. Enchantée...*" they shook hands and eyed each other, to Adam's amusement. Chloe supposed Laurence was reasonably handsome, and Laurence seemed preoccupied with Monique's breasts. An astounding pair.

"I hear Olga Pederovski is teaching you."

"That's right. Her agent is hearing me next week."

"You must have improved."

"I still can't compose, but my interpretation is good."

"I'd like to hear you sometime."

"I'm in the book."

Laurence looked up, alarm vaguely registering on his face.

"An agent? Why didn't you tell me?"

"I was going to if anything came of it."

"What might come of it?"

"He might offer me a contract and get me concert bookings."

"Are you good enough?"

"For goodness sake, you hear me all the time..."

Chloe waved her arm, knocking Laurence's glass of wine. The red liquid splashed down the front of her robe, turning the chrysanthemums an unpleasant shade of orange.

"Jesus, Chloe..."

"Oh...it'll clean."

"You can't get red wine out. It's ruined..."

She suspected he was less upset about the robe than about her performing in public, but then you could never tell with Laurence. She felt a sudden pity for him. He looked like a puppy who'd been kicked. He couldn't know how good she was. He didn't know Liberace from Richter. Adam shifted his weight to the other foot and took Monique's arm. Laurence disappeared in the crowd.

"We've got to go." He looked apologetic. "We have a dinner engagement at Claude Bissonet's. Remember him?"

"Sure. Atonality, right?"

"Middle of the road now. France Joli has recorded a few of his numbers."

"I suppose he has to eat."

"Oh no. He enjoys every minute of it. Poor Claude. But he gives terrific parties. I'll call you this week sometime. Some afternoon, all right?"

"Fine." She thought she detected an invitation in his glance, and smiled as subtly as she could. Monique seemed like the possessive type. They wouldn't last long together. Adam was looking very good to her right now, and she wondered if she was capable of deceiving Laurence. It would be so easy. The thing was, she didn't know if she wanted that sort of complication. She wanted solitude more.

She watched Adam penetrate the crowd until his curls were lost to her sight. Laurence was looking for salt to put on the stain. She knew that as certainly as she knew Laurence. He always thought he could fix things...like the trip to Greece after the abortion: naked sunbathers and women smashing the flaccid bodies of octopuses against the rocks. So Claude was writing the popular *chanson* for the popular *chanteuse*...and here was Laurence with a bottle of soda and a salt shaker....

It was unusually warm for this time of year and she could see stars above the streetlamps. Laurence held her arm a little too tightly.

"You like Adam?"

"Did I ever tell you we had an affair in my final year?"

"When you knew me?"

"At the beginning."

"I never heard of him till tonight."

"I don't think you wanted to know. I wasn't particularly secretive about it. Sometimes I came straight to your bed from him."

"That's disgusting."

"I was trying to make up my mind."

"Was sex the deciding factor?"

"No."

They turned up Simpson Avenue and she noticed the message on the church bulletin board. It read: "The Reverend Harold Peach will deliver a sermon this Sunday on the question: Do you know?"

One of life's more profound questions. Perhaps she'd go.

"Could you do do me a favour?" she asked.

"What?"

"Whenever we run into an old boyfriend of mine, you always make rather vicious love when we get home. Do you think you could try and be gentle?"

"I want you to know that I'm there."

"Believe me, I know you're there. You make me feel that I'm not...that I could be anyone with a cunt. It's not a nice feeling."

"How did he make you feel?"

"Like a part of him."

"Why did you marry me?"

He stopped and sat on the low stone wall near their home. The snow on the mountain was melting in the thaw and small rivers raced down the hillside, making the gutters glisten.

She remembered a similar night, seven years ago. She had been at Adam's flat. It was a single room filled with a lumpy hide-a-bed, a Baldwin grand, and several packing-crates. There was a closet kitchen with a fridge full of beer and leftover Chinese food, and a bathroom with cracked tiles and cockroaches. There was no bath, only a shower cubicle. The hot water was unreliable. When she arrived at Laurence's house, the house they lived in now, he was waiting with a table set in front of the fireplace, a catered dinner, chilled champagne and a proposal of marriage.

"I loved you."

"Do you still love me?"

She walked the few paces up the street to their place, and pushed open the heavy iron gate. He followed close behind.

"Well, do you?"

"Of course I do, silly. I'm here, aren't I?"

"For how long?"

She was rummaging in her purse for the keys and pre-tended she didn't hear.

He made love to her as if she were breakable, then fell asleep. She lay in bed a long while, then got up and ran a hot bath. Laurence often laughed at her, and said that all he had to do was keep her in baths and tea and she'd be happy. She washed thoroughly, removing all traces of the evening, and pulled on a nightie. It was flannel, long-sleeved and Laurence hated it. He preferred black lace. She brushed her teeth, rinsed out her mouth and exchanged the gold studs for sleepers, then turned out the light. Her head was still buzzing. She climbed the stairs to the attic. The familiar shapes of the fig tree and the piano shone in the moonlight. She sat and began to play, quietly at first, but she quickly lost herself in Debussy's moonlight. It embraced her like a lover. The crescendo lifted her, held her, and she drifted softly down with the flow of the music, sated in the dying chords.

She rose, and was about to go to bed when she realized she wasn't alone. Dimly outlined in the doorway stood Laurence. Andy was beside him, clinging to his dressing-gown. Laurence gave her a strange look, lifted Andy up and carried him downstairs. Her cheeks were burning. She walked over to the window and pressed the backs of her hands against them. She was shaking.

When she finally went down, she pushed open the door to Andy's room until a shaft of light from the streetlamp flooded across her face. The room was stuffy. She went over to the window and raised it a couple of inches. From this part of the house she couldn't see the moon or the stars, only the light shedding its harsh glare on the wet street. The pillow under Andy's cheek was damp with tears. He stirred when she sat on the bed beside him, and she rubbed his back until his breathing was regular again. In the softness of sleep, he looked like any other child. She could almost forget that he stared at her from corners, was addicted to educational television and liked his meat practically raw. In the shadows, the Lego construction took on interesting new aspects.

She was reluctant to go to bed. Laurence might still be awake and she didn't want to deal with him. Taking a cigarette from a jar on the hall table, she wandered into the bathroom.

In the dim light from the window the fixtures were soft, familiar shapes. She sat on the hamper and watched the glow at the end of her cigarette without bothering to smoke. Hanging from the shower rod was the Chinese coat. Even in the dimness an obscene blotch was visible down the front panel. Laurence had made it worse, but it wasn't his fault. None of this was his fault. He'd given her the coat and she'd accepted it: a gift.

DIMINUENDO

There is a particular children's toy that consists of various-sized gears in red, yellow and blue. If the baby gives a twist to any of the interconnected discs, the others will follow suit. In theory this should amuse the baby. The gears can be taken out and replaced with ease, altering the progression of size and colour, ostensibly to sustain the child's interest: red and yellow and blue, yellow and red and blue, blue and yellow and red; and so it goes.

It rained again today. It has rained every day for two weeks, sometimes in the morning, sometimes in the afternoon and sometimes not until night, but not a day passes that it does not rain. The pipes have backed up so often that I plug the toilet with a towel and keep the stoppers in the sinks and bathtub. There is a plague of silverfish. Joggers huffing past my window in endless progression appear oblivious to the wetness, but even the squirrels foraging through the dripping gold leaves are a bedraggled lot.

Jason spent the entire day yesterday watching football on television. He rose from the couch five times: three times to eat and drink and twice to go to the bathroom. The one time he addressed me was to ask if I had bought mustard. Jason doesn't even like football. What's the line...? "Il pleut dans mon coeur comme il pleut dans la rue." I dropped a spool of thread under the bookcase and when I reached in to fish it out, I also found two magnetic letters: a blue K and a green D. Danny and I had been like people with a stammer, who avoided certain words. We never did learn how to spell "dog." I stuck them on the fridge door, D and K, but if Jason noticed, he didn't mention it.

The rubby is sleeping in the foyer again. This morning I had to step over him to get at the newspapers. I thought perhaps he was dead, but then he grunted in his sleep and clutched his *vin rouge* a mite closer to his chest. I read an article lately claiming that the skin of grapes has strong antibiotic properties, so I suppose hypothermia poses a greater threat to the average wino than pulmonary infection.

Can you remember a time, long ago, when you entered a darkened room, saw the glow of birthday candles, and heard a hush of grownup voices before the singing began? Or the stillness of a sunlight living-room where your mother entertained a neighbour over coffee, and in which the most vivid lingering image is of the bright-red nail peelings in the ashtray? When you try to distinguish these events they dissolve from your consciousness as if they lack any basis in reality. Why do such sweet ephemerae resist examination? Why are furtive glimpses into a time of innocence all that seem possible?

Since they carted the hillside below Atwater away in great trucks, the dispossessed skunks and racoons ravage the neighbourhood garbage for their daily bread. We assumed it was cats until we saw one lumbering through the court-yard in the small hours, in the dark. One is tempted to leave out better quality trash. All things considered, I'd rather have racoons living across the street than con-dominiums.

I keep picking up hot dogs and jello. Force of habit.

Leslie phoned. She's doing a series for London Weekend Television. It's to be about three working girls who share a flat, clothes and men. They're calling it *Three's a Crowd*. I wonder if she ought to have given up the quiz show. She and Peter won £6000 at roulette one night and spent the succeeding week losing it all. I wonder if it's raining in England. It makes me think of all the old Korda movies... black umbrellas. If they lasted long enough, they might have faded to green or burgundy, but the prevailing colour was unquestionably gloomy: dour and boring black. Col-ours didn't appear until the fifties. It rained on coronation day. The showers began during the procession to Westminster and suddenly there was a flowering, a blos-soming, a burst of colour. The umbrellas were up. For some, who had endured the war and subsequent years of rationing and deprivation, that was the real crowning.

It rained overnight last Wednesday. Jason was padding

about in the pre-dawn doing paragraphs in his head when he looked out the window and saw a person lying beside the fountain in the courtyard. "This," he thought, "is not good. One can die of cold." He rifled through the kitchen in search of carbohydrates but found only a stale french loaf and a bar of Lindt chocolate. These in hand, he went down through the basement and into the rain, but on closer inspection in the creeping grey light the body was transformed into a tree stump. Jason smiled at the superintendent who stared from his window, and bit into the chocolate. When you put winter feed out for the birds you must remember to do it every day for they become dependent on it as their food source. Or so I am told.

The sound of cars passing on wet pavement is distinctly louder than the sound of cars passing on dry pavement. Moisture in the air amplifies to an excruciating level the sounds emanating from the heavy machinery currently engaged in the decimation of my street. My valium intake has increased three fold since the rains came. Inclination for outdoor activity is washed away with each succeeding downpour. The sheer quantities of mud that ooze from rents in the pavement are astonishing. One of my friends once initiated a campaign to protect the environment. His motto:

Cover it with asphalt

We neither speak nor touch, but keep distance as like poles of a magnet. Jason came in late last night, three sheets to the wind, and shut himself in the bathroom. That's where I found him in the morning, asleep on the floor, his head in the wastepaper basket. I don't know. Once we could say anything, but maybe there was nothing worth saying.

I have written and discarded two stories. One was about a very ordinary person who simply happens upon fires, and quite naturally reports them. They are all arson, and in the absence of other suspects he is arrested, convicted and sent up for ten years. The day of his release, he sees a fire, walks away, and later reads that five people burned to death. In a fit of guilt he does a self-ignition number on the steps of the Palais de Justice. The other features an idiot *savant*. His classmates at the conservatory, as a joke, fix him up with the beautiful girl he idolizes. When, early on in the evening, the realization comes to him that life is really rather nasty, he runs home, writes a sonata of stunning power and brutality, and then yells at his mother. I think I have mildew on the brain. Perhaps a litre of Chianti would help.

Rat-ta-tat-ta-tat, rat-ta-tat-ta-tat... if I shut the windows I won't be able to breathe, the radiators spew out so much damn heat. When it stops raining I'll buy some Corning Pink Fibreglass insulation and swaddle the bloody things.

The fiddler crab has taken to climbing the walls of the aquarium. She starts by scuttling up the pink-and-yellow rocks that Danny collected in his bucket at the beach two summers ago, then she disappears for a while; her angular body camouflaged in the red-brown algae accumulations on the jagged quartz that leans against the corner filter. The crab then hoists herself over the rock used to weight the filter down, and up the air-hose. At this point she loses grip and drifts to the gravel, fifteen inches below. She has been doing this for four days now. Andrew at the pet store says it is not a good sign, but declines to elaborate.

Julie wrote to say that the twins can now walk across a room, unaided. Yay twins. She is going back to work as PR officer for an electronics firm and Caspar will stay home with the boys until they are ready for nursery school. Yay Julie, yay Caspar. Will it never stop raining?

Antagon construction. Appropriately named. They are now antagonizing me by installing wide-gauge piping to service this building and the one next door. There is a trench three-quarters filled with water and mud. The front lawn looks like the Somme. When they were blowing away the hill they often blasted twenty times a day. All our walls are cracked but the landlord refuses to do anything about it. It's not in the lease. Go five feet down anywhere in Montreal and you hit bedrock. It takes one hell of a long time to dig a foundation, but once a building is up, nothing short of a direct hit will bring it down again.

Boom boom.

Jason was overnight in Ottawa. The eleven o'clock news had just concluded with a report on west-island separatists and I was concluding a fine bottle of Valpolicella '77 when I was startled by a scratching at the window and a whimpering cry. Framed in an aura from the floodlight of the seminary across the street was a small head bobbing up and down. Before I had a chance to do anything, I heard a thud and a shout. On the lawn I could see two punks kicking to a bloody pulp the thing that had been staring in the window. It was a racoon.

Jason went and hid all my valium, so I hid his pipes behind the buffet and stuffed his entire collection of Michael Foucault under the mattress.

I have taken a dislike to the wall across the street. It used to be just a nice stone wall, the back of an abandoned stable, but some upstart leasehold company has renovated the building. It had a certain architectural integrity in its ruin, but now it looks like all the travesties of Quebec style farmhouses that dot new suburbs. Next thing they'll cover the slate with asphalt roofing-tiles. There goes another jogger. They even bounce by when the mercury dips to 30 below.

We converged in the foyer at 6.30 yesterday morning: the paper boy, a construction worker who leaves his lunch there, a rubby who woke in all the scuffling and me. The paper boy, an innocent of twelve, accidentally knocked over the wino's bottle spilling the remaining contents on the white marble, like blood. The bum started screaming at the kid who dropped the newspapers on the steps and fled, while the construction worker with misguided chivalry tried to usher the rubby out of my nightgowned presence. I can't deal with scenes before my tea so I left them to their yelling and tugging. By seven the wine had been mopped up.

I took the bus over to St. Lawrence the other day where I was told I could get a really top-of-the-line espresso machine for a hundred dollars cheaper than downtown. At one stop about 30 schoolchildren piled on and the whole vehicle stank of rubber and wet wool. It yanked to a halt at Parc, and a load of books ploughed into my head. The child didn't even apologize; just giggled and plucked them off my stunned body, one by one. Meanwhile I was concussed and passing out from the smell of her perfume, "Eau de Ville LaSalle." Don't schools have dress codes anymore? What happened to tunics four inches above the knee, white blouses and hair pulled off a cleanly scrubbed face? If we had so much as hinted that we wanted to pierce our noses with safety pins....The coffee machine is a solid-looking polished steel affair, spouting an assortment of appendages. I hope Jason is pleased. Why is it that the car that whisks around the corner nearly knocking you to oblivion is always a taxi?

The lady in the next building who shares our west wall still favours Chopin above all other composers. I wish she'd play something else for a change: Bartok, Scriabin, even Bach...anything but Chopin. He's so maudlin. I've been playing Jason's John Cage records in an effort to drown her out. I never appreciated Cage before. It's amazing how well he goes along with the sound of a pneumatic drill.

When I came in from doing the groceries, the key wouldn't turn in the lock. I noticed scratchmarks on the doorframe from someone else's abortive attempts to find the keyhole. The former tenant was notorious for his associations with the local watering holes. Two elderly sisters who share the apartment opposite entered just then with a rush of damp air and came to my assistance. I doubt that the fact of my inebriation escaped them, but they are too well bred to give any indication of their disapproval. Actually, they are rather sweet. Last week, they brought over two casseroles.

Oh Lord, I want, if not a release from being, then at least a vacuum where everything is sucked out but being itself: the passage of time, the change of light and temperature, the need for sustenance, maintenance...consciousness, thought, memory. Jason sleeps on the couch every night now, and the simplest reality vanishes in a sideways glance.

I packed up Danny's room today. Jason decided that he wants a study. I sorted the clothes into different sizes and put them in plastic garbage bags for the Sally Ann, then packed the books in a crate for the twins. The toys were more difficult. Some were broken and I had to toss them.

The stuffed animals will have to be cleaned before I pass them on. I can't give away the bear with the torn ear, so I put it aside for storage. Then I flushed the fish down the toilet. The crab died last week. I may as well throw out the waggon. The wheels broke ages ago. I found an old toy at the bottom of a drawer, the gear-box. It was never a particular favourite of his; the gears simply turned, nothing more. I recall it was a christening gift, definitely not a toy that would induce me to pull $15 out of my pocket. It didn't zip when it went or pop when it stopped or whirr when it stood still...it was a toy that could bore a kid to death. If I leave it out on garbage night perhaps someone will find it; a racoon maybe, with its tiny little hands.

I had a dream last night, that Danny was crying. I went into the kitchen to fix him a bottle, and took it into his room but when I reached the bed the rubby was lying there on the Snoopy sheets and the milk had changed into wine; a real transubstantiation. I gave it to him, he said thank you, and I returned to bed. It all seemed normal in my dream. As normal as rain.

A HINGE OF POSSIBILITIES

Chloe absently placed the receiver on its cradle and leaned against the wall of the corridor. The french-doors in the living-room were rattling and the wind blew a fine low whistle through the sills. She lit a cigarette and sat on the narrow stairs, each step worn thin in the centre from generations of feet. Adam was back. Distorted in the thick round concave window, a tree bent to impossible angles, and the bricks of the garden wall dipped and twisted into the ground. A smooth jet of smoke escaped from her clenched teeth. After eighteen months he probably expected to waltz back into her life as if he were continuing a sentence.

Her stockinged foot slid over the rough slate floor of the hall and kitchen. Its warmth surprised her the same way that marble statues did when touched; as if one was surprised that the sculptor failed to instil warmth along with the impression of life. Her grey-black inanimate slate had the temperature of flesh. What if he turned up on her doorstep with suitcases? Would she show him where to unpack? When she'd moved from his apartment, she'd seen to it that the place was dusted and plants watered: she'd even continued paying half the rent until he returned from sabbatical and could make other arrangements. He'd known she wouldn't follow him, but he went anyway. So why, she thought as she butted the half-smoked cigarette, did she feel so guilty?

Maybe she'd practise the Zimmerman trio sonata. The cassette player was sitting on the bare floor beside the two pianos fitted together like a jigsaw puzzle in one corner of the large, otherwise empty room: the old rosewood Chickering that she hauled from place to place, and the austere black Baldwin, inherited, along with the money that had enabled her to buy the house, when her teacher, Olga Pederovski, died. She pushed the button on the player, and the brutal atonality of the cello and violin accompaniment assaulted her. Not in the mood. She stopped the noise. Was her dislike of contemporary works an asset? There was a detached quality to her playing that suited the music. She idled through the opening passage of a Chopin nocturne and melted into the room. Windows lined the thick walls east and west, and a huge fireplace dominated the north. The elaborate mantel was carved butternut, the same wood as the waxed windowframes and floors. The estate agent had been unable to supply the date of construction, but ventured to guess from the twenty-inch fieldstone walls and arched foundations that it was "old."

Chloe believed that it had been built by one of Montreal's religious orders as a retreat, back in the days when Westmount had been a wilderness.

The ceiling creaked and she looked at the beams that ran the length of the house. They were butternut too. Was it typical that she had never seen a butternut tree? Were there any left? The creaking stopped. Andrew, her son one weekend a month, was probably at his terminal again. What did you do with a ten-year-old one weekend a month, especially a ten-year-old who was obsessed? Against her wishes, Laurence, her ex, had actually sent him off to computer camp last summer. In an effort to draw him into a three-dimensional world, she dragged him to museums, horseback riding, apple picking, even baseball games, which she detested; but nothing could distract that face mushed against a video screen. She had offered to teach him piano, and to please her he did try though it soon became painfully obvious that he was as tone deaf as his father.

Children were one of the few things in life over which, at the outset, one naïvely expected absolute control. Chloe sat at the Baldwin, which had the stiffer action, and immersed herself in the fierce atonal study that was part of a series Adam had been working on in California. The harsh strident chords richocheted off the bare walls, the carpetless floors, the unadorned windows, and strafed the still air. A power rose within her as the force of her hands shook the piano and vibrated the thick wooden planking beneath her. This was real.

"Where are you going?" She stood up as Andrew appeared at the foot of the stairs in a half-buttoned duffel coat, lugging a knapsack. His grey eyes peered out from a fringe of pale blond hair.

"Julian asked me over. For the night too."

"And were you planning to ask my permission?"

"Sure. Can I go?"

Any baby softness had vanished sometime when she wasn't paying attention, and what stood before her was a miniature adult. She had a fleeting regret that he didn't want to spend any time with her, a greater relief that she wasn't going to be called upon to entertain. Nevertheless, she made a token effort.

"Why don't you hang around for a while, and we'll talk?"

"But Adam's coming over."

"What do you mean?"

"Well, he called last night when you were out. He said he got me some new software that isn't available up here yet."

"Why didn't you tell me?"

He shrugged and pulled his toque over his ears.

"I forgot."

"He's not coming till four. Wouldn't you like to do something together?"

"You'd rather be by yourself." He made the statement patiently, without accusation or sadness, his head cocked to one side.

"What makes you think that?"

"Jun says this is your season of solitude."

Jun was the Japanese cook-general who ran the house. She often wondered what he and Andy discussed when they were alone together.

"I beg your pardon?"

He squinted with concentration.

"Jun says that this is your time of divestment, contemplation and waiting upon a time wherein lies a hinge of possibilities."

She tried to figure this out while he shifted his weight from one foot to the other.

"Mom?"

"Yes sweetheart?"

"Can I go to Julian's now?"

"Yes...yes." Divestment, she supposed; contemplation, certainly; but waiting?

"Mom?"

"Yes dear?"

He was waiting with his hand on the doorknob.

"For the night, too?"

"Do you have your pyjamas and toothbrush?"

He nodded.

"Okay. See you tomorrow. We'll do something special."

"We don't have to."

"I want to."

He closed the door quietly, and she could hear his feet scuff on the walk and through the piles of dead leaves. He waved in at the window as he turned the corner of the house. She waved back.

Now why the hell did Sebastian call, out of the blue, demanding that she join him at the hotel for lunch? Didn't she have enough on her mind? What was the news that Bell Telephone couldn't handle? Why did he have to fly in from New York today? Chloe was about to light another cigarette and noticed that the tips of her slender fingers were yellow. She picked up the package, walked into the kitchen and emptied the contents into the trash-compacter. She liked Sebastian, but he had awful timing.

That wasn't quite true, she thought. He had discovered her at a time when her hopes for a career were stagnating. She had been living with Adam, taking in students, and playing piano at the Ritz bar, doing "Liebestraum" by request, along with other popular classics, when an interesting-looking, dark-eyed man had appeared beside her and asked her to perform Bach's Chromatic Fantasy. She glanced around the room at the elegantly turned out women and stockbrokers in three-piece suits, hesitated for a moment, then thought, "Why not?" She rubbed her hands together, warming her fingers before running the familiar path over the keyboard, and soon was oblivious to the surroundings, to the gradual hush and the pale faces turned toward her. She was also unaware that the dark man was scrutinizing her technique and appraising her impact on the impromptu audience. Waiters stopped threading between the tables, even the bartender froze. People coming in off the street hovered in the doorway, and when after thirteen minutes, Chloe rested her hands in her lap, there was a dead pause before they all rose to their feet and stunned her with enthusiastic applause. She slowly stood, bowed and fully expected to receive notice from the management. The dark man left a card identifying him as one of New York's top impressario-managers: within two months, he had overhauled her image and booked her to perform with the Baltimore Symphony Orchestra. It was Sebastian's inspiration that she dress in red, and have postmoderns comprise half her performing repertoire. He planned to base her reputation on the interpretation of contemporary works, but he knew they would never fill a hall unless the audience was presented with a selection of familiar concert pieces. Despite the fact that Stravinsky composed most of his works before 1940, most provincial audiences considered him avant-garde, and cities weren't noticeably more sophisticated. She spent about a third of her time practising Chopin, Beethoven and Brahms. Chloe spent many hours with Sebastian, and when they inevitably became lovers, it was more for convenience than passion.

As an afterthought, she turned on the trash-compacter and took pleasure in imagining the unsmokable mangle of tobacco, orange peels and milk cartons. In the mechanical hum she heard the cello section of the Zimmerman work, and thought, notwithstanding her own preference for moderns, that she was beginning to appreciate the discordant pieces Sebastian made her play. It was ironic that he was patronizing Adam as well; encouraging his composition. Neither he nor Chloe mentioned Sebastian in their letters, but each was aware of his presence in the other's life.

She shut off the machine, immediately regretting the fact that she had nothing to smoke. She'd have Jun pick some up when he did the marketing. He was kneeling over the goldfish pond in the small Victorian greenhouse abutting the kitchen, and looked up briefly to acknowledge her presence in his part of the house. Spiky yellow water-lilies drifted as aimlessly on the surface as the multicoloured carp below. His soft black crêpe de Chine cassock floated around him as he dropped frozen brine shrimp to the fish. Chloe preferred the creamy white robes that comprised his summer wardrobe. At times, he wore bright red, and although she wasn't quite sure what occasioned the change to a festive colour, she suspected religious observance. He spoke a better French than the natives, and admitted to studies in Paris, but his reticence precluded elaboration. She pictured him as a failed priest reverting to Buddhist origins. There was an air of piety about him; even when he took off in the Volkswagen, wearing jeans. She left the workings of the house entirely to him, and he consulted her only when he wished to undertake a project likely to encroach on her sensibilities; such as the construction of the goldfish pond in the greenhouse. Chloe didn't see any reason why he shouldn't have diversions, so he proceeded in his placid way to pickaxe a hole in the tile flooring, through a layer of sand and gravel, into the earth beneath, installing filter, pump, hand-pouring cement, and laying the black ceramic tiles that lined the sides and bottom of the pool. When completed, it was rectangular, two feet deep, five feet long, three-and-a-half feet wide. He stocked it with the strange goggle-eyed breed Chloe found repulsive, and sat for hours in the lotus position, staring into the water. Looking at fish was reputed to be good for the blood pressure, but she doubted his ritual was therapeutic. Then he ordered an orange tree from a nursery in Formosa, which flourished in one corner. It was small, but already bore fruit.

When Chloe first saw the greenhouse, she thought the greenhouse would be handy for growing winter tomatoes, but Jun filled the space with bright oriental poppies, crocuses, hibiscus and lavender. In one dark vaulted corner of the basement, he cultivated mushrooms in flats of decomposed horse manure, and under artificial light, an entire spice garden. He saw to it that the little wine cellar was meticulously stocked, with labels that never saw a QLB shelf. He never explained, and Chloe never asked, but simply paid the reasonable accounts presented her, and revelled in the liberation from daily banalities. The lavender was dried and sewn into sachets to keep the moths at bay, saffron was harvested from the crocuses, hibiscus blossom made an excellent soothing tea, and though she had wondered about the poppies, they were picked in flower and arranged in large blown-glass vases on the pianos. She had to admit that the flash of crimson was just what the room, otherwise devoid of colour and ornamentation, needed.

He finished feeding the fish and wafted over to the freezer where he replaced the package of shrimp.

"Jun?"

He stood quietly as she spoke.

"There will be a guest for dinner. Could you do lobster Cantonese?" She realized as she spoke, that an unconscious emphasis had been placed on the word "guest," as if she were reassuring herself that the intrusion was temporary.

Jun frowned. Had she upset some plans?

"Is that a problem?"

"No. No. That's fine. I'll go to the market later this morning."

"Too bad you didn't stock the pool with lobsters. It'd save you the trip."

He ignored her comment and ducked his head into the cupboard beside the fridge, emerging a moment later with a container of Varsol. God. He was going to do the floors again. He cherished the fourteen-inch boards more than she did, if that was possible. They were the main reason she'd bought the house. Where were the butternut trees? What did butternuts taste like? Butter? The smell of Varsol gave her a headache. She grabbed a heavy wool cape from the hall closet and passed into the living-room. When she opened the door leading into the walled garden, stray leaves were propelled across the floor by the November wind. A vine, still in flame, lingered on the leeward side of the bricks, and she gazed up at the tapering form of the ginkgo tree as she settled on the wooden deck chair. She had discovered the chair in the cellar, leaning in the shadows on the far side of an archway, and fancied it had been picked up for a song when the *Mauritania's* fittings were being auctioned off. Jun had sanded and revarnished it, and the delicate teak grain was clearly defined by the high finish. She stroked the arm with her fingertips and smiled. There was a fair breeze, and she tightened her cloak, tucking her thick black hair into the hood. The only sounds were the swish of the yellow fan leaves over the granite flagstones, and a whistling in the eaves. She might be lounging on a deck somewhere in mid-Atlantic, and soon a porter would come with tea. She could hear Jun singing old broadway tunes as he caressed the floor with rags. Birds might come if she hung suet from the branches. She'd ask Jun to pick some up....

Lunch was delivered by room-service to Sebastian's bed-side. Chloe stretched out on the pillows and noticed that the hairs on his back were unexpectedly golden in the sunlight.

"So what was so urgent that you had to rush up from New York?"

He handed her a glass of sparkling wine and joined her under the covers. The first time she had tumbled into bed with him, she had been utterly satisfied, and surprised, as she had been raised to believe that sex was inextricably tangled up with Love. It was a revelation that Like served equally well.

"So why are you here?"

"Have you ever seen a pink sailboat?"

"Don't change the subject."

"Who? Me? Never. The second Mrs. Ridley-Chase has one." He took a strategic pause and ran his finger around the rim of the wine glass. It rang in G-sharp.

"Okay. I'll bite. Who is the second Mrs. Ridley-Chase?"

"The 25-year-old cutie who snatched up the only Mr. Ridley-Chase before the first Mrs. Ridley-Chase had time to rally her defences."

"And pink sailboats?"

"Sailboat...singular. I assure you, once you've seen one ...hull, deck, sails, all pink. Peculiarly disgusting."

"Oh get on with it." She reached over to the cooler and poured more wine.

"Have you heard of the International Wildlife Fund? You have? Well there is going to be a benefit concert that's going to be on PBS Great Performances, live from Lincoln Centre, or whatever...and this sweet, misguided, over-indulged youngster happens to be on the committee. Well, we were out the other day on the aforementioned craft of the hideous hue, and she let drop that Jouri Petro-pov, in one of his renowned fits of pique, cancelled out."

"So?"

"This concert is to be a sort of mini-history of piano composition, and now there is a conspicuous dangling end where there should be a bang of post-modernism. Well, I convinced her..."

"I can guess how..."

"...that I just happened to have in my stable of performers, a terrifically talented artiste, and even though it was ridiculously short notice..."

"When is this concert?"

"Wednesday night. That even though it was ridiculously short notice, she would be able to fill in."

"Sebastian!"

"Anyway, this morning, the entertainment committee approved the selection."

Chloe clutched the bedclothes and listened to her insides rumble.

"Do you think I'm ready?"

"Of course you are, or I wouldn't have committed you. Besides, in the whole viewing audience I think only three might possibly notice if you hit a wrong note. Two if the composer is dead."

"What should I play?"

"You'll have five unaccompanied minutes. Something flashy. I want you to make an impression so I can book you for a solo debut in January, orchestra and all. You can premiere Adam's new concerto, if it's any good."

"Adam! God. What time is it?"

"2.30...relax...we have plenty of time." He took her glass, put it beside the telephone, and kissed her neck, her hair, her mouth....

Chloe was watching lobsters crawl across the kitchen floor when the bell rang. It was a real bell, solid brass suspended from an arm of iron, and it had been tugged languidly, as if the caller had been seduced by the country atmosphere of her cul-de-sac. A caller...Adam. She opened the door expectantly only to find Sebastian's familiar back. He stared at the naked maple saplings that clung to the cliff, their thin branches moving almost imperceptibly in the dying breeze. He glanced upwards as he turned to face her.

"Goya sky."

"El Greco. View of Toledo."

"Smart ass."

"Well isn't it?"

"Yes dear. But it doesn't make you any easier to live with."

He pecked her cheek en passant, and tossed his broad-brimmed fedora onto the Balwin. She slammed the door.

"You don't live with me."

"Allah be praised. Mother didn't raise me to live in a cloister. Why don't you let me buy you some furniture?"

"If I wanted furniture, I'd buy furniture. What the hell are you doing here? I thought you'd be on the plane by now."

"Where's the perfect wife? Tarring the roof? Repairing the foundations? Whipping himself up a new dress?"

He sat at the Chickering, and Chloe's muscles tensed as he flipped through her music.

"He's in the kitchen."

"Where did you find him anyway?"

"When the old lady who owned the house died, the heirs hired him to caretake while the will was in probate. It seemed logical that he stay on. Now why don't you take your hat and go?"

"Because I want to hear the new concerto."

"I don't want you here when Adam comes."

He turned a page and picked out the theme with his right hand. Chloe inhaled sharply.

"Please go."

"I'll leave after I hear the concerto." He continued playing and she wanted to hit him as he so casually abused the melody she had been sweating over.

"You'll leave then?"

"Yes."

"On your word?"

"Christ! Don't you trust me yet?"

"I'd like to."

A grey cat leapt from the garden wall to the French doors, whining and rubbing against the panes. The twilight was deep blue as Sebastian opened the door. The animal brushed past him and circled Chloe's legs, arching its back and purring loudly. She picked it up and shoved it through the cellar door.

"Bloody cat. How is it that they manage to pinpoint the very people who can't stand them, and attach themselves? Insinuating beasts."

Sebastian watched with interest as she wiped her hands on her jeans.

"Get rid of it."

"I can't. It belongs to the house."

"Aren't you going to change out of your jeans?"

"Why? Anyway, the house has weird old foundations, and if it weren't for the cat there'd be mice running over your feet. What time is it?"

"Five. Are you two getting back together?"

She threw her hands in the air, peered through the window into the gathering darkness, then pressed her palm on a switch that flooded the garden with light.

"Well, you're pretty nervous about seeing someone you won't change your jeans for."

"Oh shut up."

Chloe slapped the spotlight off and went into the kitchen. Jun was doing his meditations in the greenhouse by the light of a single candle. A faint shimmering passed in the pond. Tidy mounds of chopped food lined the dark counter, and there was a rich scent of baking. In a large pot filled with white wine the lobsters were clicking. They would pass out before being thrown in boiling water. Tender flesh. She tiptoed out. Obviously, everything was under control. She heard Adam's knock and waited in the shadows of the corridor as Sebastain let him in. After eavesdropping on the exchanged greetings, she crept up to her room, and lay on the bed for awhile, making orange circles in the blackness with the tip of her cigarette. This was her life, and she could live it any way she damn well pleased.

When she joined them twenty minutes later, Jun had lit the fire and set up the small trestle table. The two men were sitting on folding-chairs, drinking and talking. They were so relaxed. Candles were burning on the mantel, pianos and table. Sebastian smiled approvingly at the sleek black jersey dress that hugged the contours of her body, while Adam, tanned, slimmer from exercise, and perhaps a little greyer, stood to embrace her.

"Pale, beautiful Chloe. You're a sight after those blond cows. 'Age cannot wither her, nor custom stale her infinite variety.'"

Conscious of Sebastian, he kissed her lightly on the lips and handed her a glass of wine.

"Thank you Adam, for recognition of my advanced age and lack of bovinity. Sorry I kept you waiting."

Sebastian smiled sweetly.

"Waiting? Adam, were we waiting?" He winked.

"I was checking on things in the kitchen. Is that the concerto?" She indicated a fat envelope sitting on the Baldwin beside Sebastian's hat.

"Yes. Sebastian wants to hear it. Do we have time to run through it before dinner?"

Chloe noticed that the table was set for three and gave Sebastian a killing look. He grinned and shrugged.

"I suppose so."

"Here's the piano part." He delved into the package and handed her a thick pile tied with string. She was comfortable in the scenario from all the years they'd played it out. There was the familarity of the hands she'd known for fifteen years, since she took his course at McGill, fumbling with the knot in the cord. She wanted to touch his hands.

"I haven't quite polished the orchestral transcription, yet, but that should take only a couple of weeks. After that, it shouldn't take me too long to get copies printed up... again another week or two, maybe longer, since it'll be around Christmas. It's scored for about 40 instruments. I hope that's enough time...provided, of course, you like it."

As they spread papers over their respective pianos, she suddenly realized he wasn't addressing her. She beckoned Sebastian with a snap of her fingers.

"I need you to turn pages. I'll nod."

It was strange seeing Adam's curly head at the other piano. Sebastian stood attentively by as they limped through the first movement; Adam conducting her with tosses of his head. By the second movement, she was swept into the flow of the simple repetitive theme, more melodic than his usual compositions. It was a startling change from the style of the studies; derivative of people like Takemitsu, but this had a unique quality, with no identifiable influence. The only thing it came close to was the later work of Scriabin. There was an impressionistic flavour that would make it accessible to the concert-going public. With the completion of the allegro section, she recognized that Adam had finally developed into a first-rate composer. The final chords still hung in the air as she threw her arms around him. Over his shoulder she saw the dedication at the head of his copy: *For Chloe* and her body began to mould itself to his as he returned the hug. The feeling of claustrophobia overcame her and she pushed him away.

"I'll see about dinner."

"I'll help."

"You needn't bother. I'm quite capable." There was a sharpness to her tone she immediately regretted, seeing Adam's puzzled expression. Sebastian was watching with a bemused smile as he drank the diluted remains of his Scotch. She wanted to kick him out but didn't have the nerve. Adam followed her into the corridor and pressed her against the wall.

"What is going on? Is it Sebastian?"

His tan accentuated the fan of creases radiating from the corners of his eyes, and she was momentarily weakened by the scent of Gauloises on his clothes. It would be so easy to get into all that again. He suited her like silk.

"Nothing's going on. He manages my career. I manage my life."

"And what is your life right now? Why didn't you come with me?"

"Why did you leave?"

"I needed a change...for my work. You never visited. Your letters were so...impersonal."

"Maybe I needed a change...for myself." She edged over and sat on the stairs. He remained standing.

"Are you punishing me for going?"

"No. But when you told me you were leaving, I knew I had to make a choice. It occurred to me that I had never, in my entire life, been alone. It was a chance to get a perspective on things. Us, me, my work."

"That's pretty calculating."

His face was filled with anger and longing. Chloe didn't think she'd ever understand men.

"I saw your concert at Berkeley."

Small shock. She hadn't told him she was going to

California. How to brazen this one through? She studied his feet. Leather jogging shoes.

"I just happened to see a copy of the Berkeley student newspaper, and there you were on the back cover. I drove up that day, to see you."

"Why didn't you come backstage? It would have been lovely to see a familiar face. Touring is pretty lonely."

"Don't try and pull that on me. I'm not your cousin."

"I didn't mean..."

"Why didn't you call? We could have arranged some time together."

His feet were disappearing in a black haze.

"I don't know. It didn't occur to me. I was busy..."

"When people are in love they remember, they make time." He leaned over and was digging his fingers into her shoulders.

"You're hurting me."

He let go and pounded the wall with his fist.

"Do you love me?"

She hugged her knees and didn't answer, wanting to bury her face in his shabby old tweed suit. One of the few domestic efforts of her life was sewing leather patches on the worn elbows.

"I resigned from McGill. I'm taking a job at the music faculty of UCLA beginning next fall."

"I wondered why you didn't come back in August."

"I'm heading back as soon as I sublet the flat and ship my stuff."

"I suppose you have someone there?"

"What?"

"You know...a woman..." She needed a smoke.

"No, Chloe. I don't. Shit! I think you'd be relieved if I did. What's happened to you?"

"Adam, please...look, I do love you."

"Then come with me."

"I can't."

"You can if you want to. You can pursue your career from anywhere. All you have here is an empty house, for God's sake."

"It's not empty."

"Two pianos and a dishwasher?"

She pushed past him into the kitchen where Jun was arranging the lobster Cantonese on a bed of rice. He ignored their entrance and carried the platter into the living-room. Chloe went to the other side of the goldfish pond while Adam stood in the archway.

"There's Andrew..."

"Come off it. Laurence'd let you have him three months a year, if you wanted him, which you don't!"

Ouch.

"Well maybe I don't want you either. I definitely don't want California...or New York."

He winced.

"That's right. Sebastian's been bugging me to locate there for nearly a year. Well I'd rather stay here, thank you. I like stagnating cities. Perhaps when I tire of Montreal, I'll move to Berlin!"

"Chloe..."

"This is my home. Not my parents', not Laurence's, not yours. The deed is in my name. I pay the taxes. When the roof leaks, I call the contractors. The place is empty because it's not cluttered up with someone else's leavings. I'll get bloody chairs when I'm good and ready, and when I do, they'll be more than just places to sit!"

"Jesus...calm down."

"Give me a cigarette."

He lit her one and walked over to the pots of hibiscus leaning on the shelving beside her. She inhaled and tried to think logically. He was standing so close she could feel his warmth through two layers of clothing. She belonged. She didn't want to belong.

"Adam, I'm 35 years old, and am only now learning who I am. I don't want to be encased in anyone else's life."

"Encased? Was sharing a life with me so stultifying?" Adam turned suddenly, upsetting a pot of flowers. A clot of dirt fell in the pond, disturbing the fish.

"I'm sorry all this is hurting you. I don't want to hurt you. If it hadn't been for you I'd probably still be living a cushy, deadening life with Laurence. I know a couple who have been together for twenty years, and one day, he told me he was happy she had her little passion...I mean, this woman is a respected art historian who does consulting work for places like the National Gallery...because she was more contented than if she merely messed about the house. God! I got the impression he would have been happier if she preferred doing just that. That benign patronizing attitude. Men think they're being so magnanimous. Even when I was living with you, it was your work that was serious. My involvement with the piano was a quasi-diversion as far as you were concerned. Where people were concerned, I was your "lady." Laurence and Chloe, Adam and Chloe...Siamese twins...and no matter how unstructured the relationship, obligations develop...expectations. You looked to me for entertainment; I always had to be on. Have you any idea how taxing that was? It was almost easier living with Laurence. He only expected me to be decorative."

Adam listened silently. She ground her butt in a pot.

"It's the same when I perform...you saw the schtick... the red dress, the split program: 'The stunning Chloe Delaney breezes through both classic and contemporary works with style and panache. This critic predicts a brilliant future for the lady.' They see me on stage and want me to behave a certain way, and despite all my efforts at detachment, I wind up acting out parts, playing whatever

Chloe they're fantasizing. I get so wired, I don't know what's true anymore. That's why I need this house, do you see?"

"But you claim to love me?"

"You aren't listening. This has nothing to do with love... it has to do with survival. Maybe someday I'll be prepared to live with someone, but right now I can't. I won't."

"Is that it then? All over...no more?"

Chloe took the cigarette he had just lit and stared at their two pairs of feet.

"I want you. I just don't want to live with you."

"That's not good enough."

"Can we still be friends?"

Adam clenched his fists, glared at her for about 30 seconds, then abruptly left the room. She was supporting herself against a shelf of flats when the front door slammed. The hand holding the cigarette shook. Divestment....

Sebastian sat in solitary splendor behind a pot of hyacinths Jun had force-bloomed. When Chloe came into the light he offered to serve her dinner.

"I'm not in the least bit hungry. Pour me some wine, would you? Oh, never mind." She returned to the counter in the short corridor and poured herself a cognac. Sebastian continued eating as she sat down opposite. He said nothing.

"Sebastian?"

He looked up, still chewing.

"Do you like November?"

He patted his mouth with the napkin then folded his hands on the edge of the table.

"Not really. I like skiing, and there's rarely any snow."

"No. I mean the feel of November; the melancholy."

"I can't recall any mood exclusive to the month...inherent as it were. Is this a trick question?"

"But don't you find it odd? Like a fifth season, hovering in a static nether region, neither autumn nor winter....Its subtlety, austerity...fields muted with frost...trees drenched black against undecided skies....'"

"Like I said, I prefer snow. You know, one of the chief traits I've always admired about you was your utter lack of sentimentality. I can't tell you how your little speech depresses me. Shall we change the subject?"

She handed Sebastian the empty snifter, which he dutifully rose to refill.

"I thought the concerto was excellent. It's a real advance for Adam."

"Don't count on him letting me perform it. I think I'm in his black book."

"Rubbish. A temporary sting. Even on the outside chance that he detests you, which I doubt, he's not going to stop his work being performed to an audience of New York critics simply to spite you."

"Oh yeah?"

"He is, in his own way, as ambitious as you."

Chloe digested that idea while Sebastian stoked the fire.

"Where's Jun?" she asked.

"In the basement, clearing out mouse carcasses, I think."

"Do you think I'm awful?"

"Not at all."

"Do you think it's going to snow?"

"No."

"Do you...oh hell. If you don't want to witness a maudlin number, you'd better leave."

"Play me something."

"Not now Sebastian."

"Mozart...no...Scarlatti."

"I'm not in the mood."

"Sonata in G Major. You used to play that a lot."

"That was before you started cramming post-modern

crap down my throat."

"That's work. Play the Scarlatti for me. Go on...."

Chloe reluctantly put down the brandy and pushed the chair out. He leaned back on his and stretched his legs.

"The Chickering. I prefer the tone for classical."

She brushed her fingers over the fine grain of the polished rosewood. She loved this piano.

"It's a fluke. It has a wafer-thin sounding-board of cypress, and the most gorgeous action. You only have to think the notes. My tuner's been trying to buy it from me for years."

"Shall I turn pages?"

Chloe smoothed her dress beneath her as she settled on the stool and warmed her fingers. The fire and candlelight flung shadows the length of the room, glowing on the warm floor and Sebastian's glossy hair. She realized she was smiling.

"Later, perhaps. I know this one by heart."